cover colors by
GUY MAJOR

lettering by
BRYAN LEE O'MALLEY

"Blue Belles" and short gags lettering by
CHYNNA CLUGSTON

book design by
KEITH WOOD

schm
JAM

Published by Oni Press, Inc.
JOE NOZEMACK publisher
JAMES LUCAS JONES editor in chief
RANDAL C. JARRELL managing editor
DOUGLAS E. SHERWOOD editorial assistant
JILL BEATON editorial intern

This collects the Oni Press *Blue Monday* comic books *Dead Man's Party*, *Lovecats*, and *Nobody's Fool*, as well as short material from various sources.

Editorial soundtrack: The Coral, *Magic & Medicine*; illicit Suede MP3s from Summer 2003 concerts; Tricky's cover of "The Love Cats"

ONI PRESS, INC.
6336 SE Milwaukie Avenue, PMB30
Portland, OR 97202
USA

www.onipress.com
www.bluemondaycomics.com

First edition: September 2003
ISBN-13: 978-1-929998-66-X
ISBN-10: 1-929998-66-X

3 5 7 9 10 8 6 4 2
PRINTED IN CANADA.

To Jon,

For all the Moonpies and Pennywhistles.

"Dead Man's Party"

HEY, ERIN!
TRICK OR TREAT!!!
HEY! WELCOME TO THE HOUSE O' FUNGUS!

Erin's Halloween party was in full effect. A ton of kids had shown up, clad in frighteningly tacky costumes and eating dangerous amounts of Candy Corn. All agreed that the punch rocked, that the vienna sausages ruled, and that even though Monkeyboy left a big stinky log floating in the toilet that stunk up the house for about an hour, they were having a fabulous time...

...That is, until the biggest storm in eighty-eight years hit the Fresburger/Deadwood area, and all their parents came to pick them up.
All except a handful. A sad, pathetic crew they were.

A devil.
A pirate.
A flapper stuffed with little vienna sausages.
SIGH
And three Kubrickian hooligans (they couldn't find a fourth).
NO LIGHTS, NO TELEVISION, NO MUSIC! MY PARTY TOTALLY RUINED... GOD!!!
THE SPECIALS "GHOST TOWN"
AND THE LITTLE VIENNA SAUSAGES ARE COLD NOW. WHAT ARE WE GOING TO DO?
SOB
HEY, THIS RADIO ACTUALLY HAS FRESH BATTERIES IN IT. WE CAN HEAR THE NEWS...
BLACKOUTS IN FRESBURGER, CLOVEN, PANDALE, RAYDBLUD, DEADWOOD...
SORRY, KIDS-- HALLOWEEN ACTIVITIES HAVE BEEN SHUT DOWN FOR THE REST OF THE NIGHT. THERE IS A CURFEW AS A RESULT OF THE BLACKOUT.
WOW, THIS IS PRETTY BAD, HUH? LIGHTNING, CURFEWS, BLACKOUTS -- AND ON SAMHAIN OF ALL DAYS!
IT'S TOO SPOOKY, WHAT WITH IT BEING THE DAY THAT THE VEIL BETWEEN OUR WORLD AND THE SPIRIT REALM IS AT ITS THINNEST...
DON'T TELL ME YOU BELIEVE THAT SHIT!
OF COURSE I DO, BECAUSE IT'S TRUE!
SPIRITS WANDER AROUND THE EARTH ON HALLOWE'EN-- WHICH IS WHY THE CELTS INVENTED JACK-O'-LANTERNS AND LIT CANDLES AND PLACED THEM IN WINDOWS, ALL IN ORDER TO GUIDE THE GHOSTS, AND THEY USED TO LEAVE OFFERINGS OF FOOD AND SET EXTRA CHAIRS AT THEIR TABLES FOR THEIR DEPARTED LOVED ONES, AND PEOPLE DRESSED IN DISGUISES IN ORDER TO TRICK MISCHIEVOUS NATURE SPIRITS AFTER DARK! DUH! DID YOU KNOW JACK-O'-LANTERNS USED TO BE MADE OUT OF TURNIPS?
← LOVES BOOTY.

YOU'RE JUST THE QUEEN OF USELESS INFORMATION, AREN'T YOU?
NOW THAT I THINK OF IT, LET'S BLOW OUT ALL THE JACK-O'-LANTERNS BEFORE IT'S TOO LATE! IF I SEE A GHOST TONIGHT, I'LL TOTALLY LOSE MY SHIT!
IF YOU'RE SO BIG ON HALLOWEEN, BLEU, HOW CAN YOU BE SO AFRAID OF GHOSTS ALL THE TIME?
BECAUSE THEY'RE FUCKIN' SCARY, CLOVER!
HAVEN'T YOU EVER SEEN THE ENTITY???
WELL, DON'T WORRY, FINNEGAN.
AT THE WORST YOU MIGHT COME ACROSS THE GHOST OF ERIN'S DITHERING, BIBLE-BANGING, NEWSPRINT-SNIFFIN' GREAT GRANDDAD OR SOMETHING, BUT THAT'S ABOUT IT.
YEAH... I GUESS YOU'RE RIGHT. I'M JUST BEING SUPERSTITIOUS, AS USUAL, I GUESS.
I KNOW HOW YOU ARE. YOU SURE YOU DON'T WANT ME TO BLOW OUT THE JACK-O'-LANTERNS SO YOU CAN KEEP YOUR SANITY?
NO... I PROMISE I WON'T FREAK OUT ABOUT THEM. IF ANY GHOSTS SHOW UP, I'LL JUST PRETEND THEY DON'T EXIST, OKAY?
BOO
KNOCK KNOCK KNOCK
COOL! I'LL GET IT!
I THOUGHT THERE WAS A CURFEW. THERE'S STILL TRICK-OR-TREATERS?
HAPPY HALLO--
--WEEN?!
ZOOP ZOOP
ZOOP!!!
AAAAAAAAAAAAAAAAAAAAAAAAAAAAAAA

I CAN'T BELIEVE THIS SHIT! YOU GUYS ARE GOING TO MAKE A LIAR OUT OF ME, I TOLD THEM I WOULDN'T FREAK OUT TONIGHT!
DEVYL
ZOOP!
YOU ALL RIGHT, BLEU??
OH, YEAH! EVERYTHING'S COOL!
DIDN'T SOUND THAT WAY.
TCH. CHICKS ARE ALWAYS PULLING STUNTS LIKE THAT, TRYIN' TO GET PEOPLE TO RUN TO THEIR RESCUE.
I'M A-OKAY. NO PROBLEM HERE! JUST JOKIN' AROUND. HEH!
BLEU, SURE Y'AINT HIDIN' SOMETHIN'?
fidget fidget
NO, NOTHING!
WELL, ALL RIGHT.
MWA-HA HA-HA
ZOOP!
WELL, COME ON, THEN. WE GOTTA FIGURE OUT WHAT TO DO WITH THE REST OF YOUR HOLIDAY.
OKAY.
GET BACK DOWN, YOU GUYS!
GRR!

I HAD AN IDEA FOR WHAT TO DO.
WE'RE GOING TO HAVE A SCARY STORY CONTEST-- YOU KNOW, LIKE MARY SHELLEY AND LORD BYRON DID ALMOST TWO HUNDRED YEARS AGO!
THE CURE "THE WALK"

THAT'S A DUMB IDEA, SCARY STORIES ARE RETARDED.
SHUT IT, ALAN. THAT'S A GREAT IDEA! HOW LONG DO WE GET TO WRITE THE STORIES?
A HALF HOUR. I HAVE PAPER, PENS, AND CANDLES FOR YOU GUYS, SO FIND YOUR OWN ROOMS AND GET BUSY, AND I'LL SET THE TIMER. LET'S GO!

And so the children retreated to their chambers and constructed the most frightening stories they could think of.
BWRRRR
SNORT
...

Or tried to, at least.

And thus began the scare-fest!
OKAY, COUNTER CLOCKWISE-- YOU START, VICTOR.
ALL RIGHT, MY TALE IS ONE OF THE UNDEAD!
NO! NOT THAT...!
AH, NO WAY! HA-HA-HA! YOU'RE AFRAID OF ZOMBIES?
TOTALLY SCARED OF HORROR STORIES/FILMS
NO, I JUST DON'T LIKE 'EM IS ALL. THEY'RE... BORING. TOTALLY UNREALISTIC. THE MOVIES ARE ALL THE SAME, YOU KNOW.
YOU LIE, THEY GIVE YOU NIGHTMARES, DON'T THEY?! YOU BIG PUSSY!

SHUT UP, THEY DO NOT!
POUT POUT POUT
QUIET! LET VICTOR TELL HIS STORY. GO AHEAD, VICTOR.
IT WAS WHAT APPEARED TO BE A TYPICAL OCTOBER AFTER-NOON IN DEADWOOD, CALIFORNIA.
THEY JUST HIRED THIS NEW GUY AT LUCKY BURGER, AND THE MAN-AGER WAS SHOWING HIM THE ROPES...
LUCKY BURGER
"HEY, I WORK AT LUCKY BURGER!"
"YEAH, MONKEYBOY, AND THE GUY LOOKS A LOT LIKE YOU TOO. SO, ANYWAY..."
...AND YOU TAKE THE FROZEN FRIES AND DUNK 'EM IN LIKE THIS. THEN YOU SWITCH BACK TO THE BURGERS, AND FLIP 'EM. GOT IT?
YEAH. BUT, WHAT ABOUT THE SECRET SAUCE?
WELL, THE SECRET SAUCE USED TO BE RANCH DRESSING AND ORANGE MARMALADE, BUT THEY SAID THEY WERE GOING TO IMPROVE IT AND SEND US NEW STUFF SOON.
I GUESS THIS IS IT, SINCE WE GOT THIS BIG SHIPMENT IN THIS MORNING. WE'RE GOING TO START USING IT TO-DAY.
WOW, THOSE ARE HUGE CANS!
YEAH. NO PAPERWORK CAME WITH IT, BUT IT SAYS TOP SECRET ON THE SIDE, SO THIS HAS TO BE THE NEW SAUCE.
TOP SECRET
IN CASE OF EMERGENCY
CALL 1-800-555-66
ASK FOR COLONEL BU
WASH THEM MITTS. IT'S THE LAW
YOU WANNA BE THE FIRST TO TRY SOME? HERE, STICK THIS SPIGOT INTO THE SIDE.
SURE!
IT WAS HARD TO GET IN THERE, BUT I FINALLY MADE IT WORK! LOOK, BOSS, THE SAUCE IS GREEN!
YEAH, AND IT GLOWS, TOO! LET'S EAT SOME!
WOW, THAT WAS GOOD. TASTED REAL MINTY AND MEATY!
WELL, WE BETTER GET BACK TO WORK. YOU TAKE OVER THE REGISTER, I GOTTA HIT THE CAN. I THINK I GOT THE SQUITS.
YEAH, OKAY. HURRY UP, THOUGH, MAN. I MUSTA ATE TOO MUCH, I FEEL A LITTLE PUKEY.
I'M FOKIN' HUNGRY!
YEAH, ME TOO, BUT WE DON'T HAVE ANY MONEY.
MONKEYBOY JUST GOT A JOB AT LUCKY BURGER. MAYBE YOU GUYS CAN GET SOME FREE FOOD FROM HIM?
YEAH, LET'S GO!
THAT KID DOWN THE STRE
SKINS SMEL

I'D LIKE A LUCKY BURGER COMBO, WITH EXTRA SECRET SAUCE PLEASE, JUST LIKE THE TWENTY PEOPLE BEFORE ME ORDERED.
SURE. THAT'LL BE TWO DOLLARS AND FIFTY--
BRAAAAIIINS...!
EXCUSE ME? HOW MUCH?
I SAID, TWO DOLLARS AND FIFTY--
BRAAAAAIIINS!
OHHH, NOOO...
I HOPE NO ONE SAW THAT. I'D GET A WARNING FOR SURE.
I BETTER PUT THE BODY OUT BACK...
HELLO? MONKEY-BOY? YOU IN THERE SOMEWHERE?
WHAT'S WITH ALL THESE PEOPLE? THEY DON'T LOOK SO GOOD.
I GOTTA GO TO THE BATHROOM, I'LL BE BACK IN A SECOND.
MAYBE THE FLU IS GOING AROUND. WE SHOULD EAT OUR FOOD NEXT DOOR IN THE CEMETERY SO WE DON'T CATCH ANYTHING.
OOOH, HEY...GUYS. WHAAAT'S UP...
DUDE, YOU LOOK LIKE YOU'RE GONNA HURL, YOU ALL RIGHT?
Hey, Clover-- you sure you still want to eat here? I mean, if the flu is going around, the food might be covered with those germs...
I gotta eat, I'm fekkin' starving.
I ALREADY PUKED MY GUTS OUT A WHILE AGO. THEY'RE IN THE SINK.
BRAINS
WE WERE WONDERING IF YOU COULD KICK DOWN SOME FREE FOOD?
SUUUURE. WHAT DO YOU WANT TO EAT--
BRAAAAIIINS?
HA-HA, NO... JUST GIMME A LUCKY BURGER COMBO.
ME TOO.
WHAT ABOUT YOU GUYS? BURGERS?
BRAAAAIINS?
NAH, DUDE. WE'RE GOOD.
AAAAAHH!!!!!!!!
GET OFF ME, FREAK!!
WHAT THE HELL!?
JESUS, SOME GUY IN THE MEN'S ROOM JUST BIT MY ARM! I THINK HE WAS TRYING TO GO FOR MY CROTCH OR SOMETHING!
POOPER
THAT MUST BE WHERE YOUR BRAAAAIIIINS ARE. ORDER'S READY.
WHAT'S GOING ON?
WE'RE GETTING THE FUCK OUT OF HERE, THAT'S WHAT'S GOING ON!
THIS PLACE SMELLS LIKE PEPPERMINT MEATLOAF, AND I JUST CAN'T HANDLE THAT SHIT!
BRAAAAIIIINS.
MONKEYBOY, MEET US AT THE CEMETERY AFTER WORK, OKAY?

www.phillyburbs.com/halloween2000/zombies/zombiesdo.shtml

"TOP SECRET"? HEY, THAT'S A NUMBER FOR CONTACTING THE ARMY!
AND THIS AIN'T FILLED WITH HAMBURGER SAUCE! LOOK! A CORPSE!
THIS MUST MEAN THAT THE BODIES WERE CONTAMINATED WITH SOME SORT OF CHEMICAL THE GOVERNMENT WAS EXPERIMENTING WITH NEAR AN ANCIENT INDIAN BURIAL GROUND THAT MADE THE CORPSES MOVE AND EAT PEOPLE, AND THE PAPERS FOR THE PLACE THEY WERE SUPPOSED TO BE SHIPPED TO MUST HAVE GOTTEN MIXED UP WITH SOME GENERAL'S LUNCH ORDER! WE HAVE TO TELL THE GANG!
BUT WHY WERE THOSE ZOMBIES SCREAMING "BRAAAIINS"?
BECAAAAUSE...
THAT'S THE ONLY THING THAT MAKES THE PAIN STOP.
WE CAN SEE THAT NOW.
YOU GRAB THAT BASEBALL BAT WITH THE SPIKE THROUGH IT NEXT TO YOU, AND I'LL GRAB THE EMERGENCY AXE! LET'S MUTILATE SOME ZOMBIE ASS!
RIGHT!
I WASN'T GONNA EAT YOUR BRAINS, I JUST WANTED TO GIVE YOU A WET WILLEH!
DIE AGAIN!!!
BUT I DIDN'T EAT MY BURGER! URK!
VIIIICTOR...
UHH!
COME HERE, VICTOR... LET ME GIVE YOU A WET WILLY...
SUUUUURE.
GIMME THAT!
TURNING INTO A ZOMBIE DOESN'T MEAN YOU HAVE TO TURN INTO A SLUT!
AW, YOU RUINED A PERFECTLY GOOD ZOMBIE BABE!
SHUT UP! CALL THE NUMBER ON THE SIDE OF THAT TANK!
CHOP
GO, SHE-RA!

CALLING THAT NUMBER ISN'T GOING TO SAVE YOU FROM ME.
BEEP Hello and welcome to Moviefone, brought to you by Kixy 95.7--
SORRY! HABIT!

HA-HA-HA... GIRLS CAN'T HURT ZOMBIES, DON'T YOU KNOW THAT?

MAN, CAN'T YOU JUST GO TO THE STORE AND BUY COW BRAINS?
WHY SHOULD I HAVE TO *BUY* THEM WHEN I HAVE FREE ONES RIGHT IN FRONT OF ME?

YOU FUCKIN' SUCK, THAT WAS COLD.
BUT THIS IS HOT, AND JUST FOR YOU, ALAN!
HUH?

GOTTA KEEP AT LEAST ONE BABE ALIVE!
THANKS, VICTOR!

GOSH, YOU'RE SO GREAT! YOU TOTALLY SAVED MY LIFE!
CHOP

HOPEFULLY TWICE. I CALLED THE NUMBER AND THEY SAID THEY WERE SENDING HELP RIGHT AWAY, SO MAYBE THEY'LL GET HERE BEFORE THE REST OF THE ZOMBIES BREAK IN!
WHAT?
BUT OF COURSE, YOU REALIZE WHAT THAT COULD MEAN...

THAT WE MIGHT NOT BE SAVED! SO IN OUR LAST PRECIOUS MOMENTS WE SHOULD TAKE THE TIME TO HAVE REALLY KINKY SEX, SINCE IT'LL PROBABLY BE OUR LAST CHANCE!
OKAY!
WHATEVER!
"GOD, VICTOR... YOU HAVE NO SHAME!"

IT'S JUST A STORY!
AND YOU EVEN MOSTLY RIPPED IT OFF FROM OUR FAVORITE ZOMBIE MOVIE-- YOU'RE NOT SUBTLE, YOU KNOW! *
* See *Blue Monday: Lovecats* for details!

HEY, EVERYBODY BORROWS FROM EVERYBODY! DON'T BLAME ME!
WHY'D I HAVE TO BE A ZOMBIE? WHAT IS THE *MEANING*?
ALAN, WHO'S YOUR GIRLFRIEND? SHE A GOOD KISSER?

WHAT? NO! ... SHUT UP!

YOU GONNA HAVE BAD DWEEMS NOW, LITTLE MAN?
FUCK YOU!
OH, SHIT. WHERE'D THE JESUS HEADS GO?

WHERE COULD THEY BE... WHERE COULD THEY BE...?

GASP

PUSH PUSH PUSH

NO!!!
WHAT IN THE NAME O'GOD--?

MAN, I REALLY HAVE TO KEEP AN EYE ON THEM!
THEY WERE GOING TO PUSH THIS ONTO YOUR HEAD!
WHAT? WHO WERE?
I DIDN'T SEE ANY-THING.

THE-THE... NEVER MIND.
ALL RIGHT, BLEU! HALLU-CINATING AGAIN?
IT'S YOUR TURN, SPAZ.

PUT THE FUCKIN' LOTION IN THE CASKET!!!

"With Valerie still frightened by what had happened, Christie Colvin decides to go out and look for Gregory in the early hours of the evening."
GREGORY, IF Y'DON'T COME OUT SOON, I'LL BEAT YA FOKIN' SILLY!

>sniff< GREGORY?
YOU FORGET TO WIPE, OR SOME-THIN'?

GREGORY, YOU DON'T LOOK SO WELL...

WHERE'S CHRISTIE?
DOES SOMEONE NEED TO GO FIND *HER* NOW, INSTEAD OF LOOKING FOR GREGORY?
HAVE BILLY DO IT.
I CAN'T. I FIRED HIS DUMB ASS EARLIER TO-DAY...HE WAS AFTER A PIECE OF VALERIE AGAIN.
KNOCK KNOCK KNOCK

"An unexpected visitor arrives!"
YES?
SORRY TO BOTHER YOU, MA'AM. I'VE COME A LONG DIS-TANCE TO MEET MY AMERICAN RELATIVES...
I'M THE FIRST COUSIN OF...ELEANOR COLVIN...A DESCENDANT OF RUPERT.
DID WE COME AT A BAD TIME?
REEK REEK
I'M SORRY... ONE OF MY GIRLS IS MISSING, AND OUR GOVERNESS WAS FRIGHTENED BY YOUR BILLY EARLIER--
BUT PLEASE, COME INSIDE FOR A WHILE... MINT?
BILLY! WHAT ARE YOU DOING HERE?

WELL, I--
THANK YOU. BILLY SAID HE WAS OUT OF WORK, AND I NEED A SERVANT FOR MY NEW HOME.
I'VE ARRIVED TO CLAIM THE HOUSE MY BELOVED ANCESTOR LEFT ME.

YOU MEAN, THAT DILAPI-DATED OLD HOUSE ON THE EDGE OF THE ESTATE?
YOU DON'T WANT BILLY TO HELP YOU, HE'S A COMPLETE JACKASS.
PRECISELY.
HEY, DICK!

NOW, NOW! DON'T FORGET YOUR MANNERS, SLAVE!
OW! AAAGH! YOU BAS-TAAARD!
ON SECOND THOUGHT, MAYBE YOU SHOULD KEEP HIM--FOR A REALLY, REALLY LONG TIME.

I HAVE THE ORIGINAL PAPERS LOCKED AWAY, BUT I'LL BRING THEM FOR YOU TO LOOK OVER.
I HAVE NO URGE TO MAKE YOU UNCOMFORTABLE, DEAR COUSIN. I'D LOVE NOTHING MORE THAN TO LIVE HARMONIOUSLY--
THE RESEM-BLANCE IS REMARK-ABLE...
Why don't you shut up and have another mint before you kill us, assho--

--ON THIS LOVELY PROPERTY WITH MY BLOOD RELATIVES.
OOF!
BOOT
WHAT'S WITH THE MINTS?! MY BREATH SMELLS FABULOUS!
IT'S A SUBTLE HINT FOR OUR ASTUTE READERS, ALAN! IT LETS THEM KNOW YOU'RE PLAYING A *VAMPIRE*, SINCE VAMPIRES ARE FAMOUS FOR HAVING SHIT FOR BREATH!

"Gregory was already back at home safe in his bed when Christie was found later that night--with minor puncture wounds on her neck. She was put to bed and examined by a doctor, who was positive she'd be feeling much better in time for the Colvins' Autumn Costume Ball the following evening."
SMELLY... SO SMELLY...
"The unexpected visitor was invited to be their guest that night, and all the preparations had been made..."
PERCY FAITH "THEME FROM A SUMMER PLACE"
WELL, WELL, WELL. IT FEELS JUST LIKE HOME AGAIN. FETCH ME SOME MORE MINTS, BILLY.
THEY AREN'T HELPING THE STENCH, SERIOUSLY...
SHUT UP AND GET ME MY GODDAMN WINTERGREEN CERTS, YOU TWIT!!!
OW! OWW! GAAAD!!
YOU'VE MADE IT, I SME-- SEE! SEE.
YES, IT'S A LOVELY SOIREE.
EUURGH, IT'S THE SABRE-TOOTHED STINKY-MAN.
ERM... LET ME INTRODUCE YOU TO CHRISTIE, THE MOST VIBRANT OF THE COLVINS...
"Dude, you're supposed to be entranced by him, you two have bonded! You're in LOVE with him! Even though he brushes you off in a second..."
WHAAAT? NO FOKIN' WAY. LIKE I'D EVER WANT HIM, AND AS IF HE COULD EVER BE CHOOSY.
EXCUSE ME? I COULD HAVE MY PICK OF THE LITTER, BABY, AND YOU KNOW IT! ALL THE KITTENS WANT MY MILK!
"It's a STORY! Just pretend, okay?! And Alan, your 'milk'? That's fuckin' gross."

OKAY, OKAY, AHEM.
OOOH, IT'S THAT DEAD SEXY MAN-MUFFIN, THE VAMPIRE!
GOSH, I WISH HE'D POKE MY THROAT WITH HIS LONG, HARD FANG AGAIN!
FANGS! FANGS!! PLURAL!
YEAH, YEAH, YEAH!!!
HUMP HUMP HUMP
OFF WITH YOU, WENCH!
BOOT
I SEE YOU TWO HAVE ALREADY... MET.
ER, AND HERE'S OUR YOUNG GREGORY'S GOVERNESS, VALERIE STRIDE--
AH, NOW THIS IS MORE LIKE IT. HOW DO YOU DO, MY LOVELY? WHAT A BEAUTIFUL, SILKY THROAT YOU HAVE...
H-HELLO...
WHATEVER! "HI, I'M ALAN, CAN I MAKE YOUR SILKY THROAT MILKY?"
MINTS
BLEU, WHERE'S ALL THE BLOOD? I'M FALLING ASLEEP.
THIS ISN'T ALL ABOUT GORE, YOU KNOW!
YAWN
VAMPIRES AREN'T SCARY. SLASHERS ARE SCARY.
WHY DO I HAVE TO BE THE SLOB THAT GETS BEAT UP?
THAT BLOWS!
EVEN ALAN ISN'T FREAKED OUT BY YOUR STORY.
HOW CAN I BE? SHE'S RIPPING OFF DARK SHADOWS! HELL, MY PARENTS USED TO WATCH RERUNS OF THAT BORING CRAP RIGHT AFTER GENERAL HOSPITAL.
WAIT! IT GETS BETTER--
VETO!!
YOU'RE THE ONLY ONE WHO THINKS CLASSIC SHITE LIKE WUTHERING HEIGHTS IS FRIGHTENING THESE DAYS, BLEU.
YOU'RE SUCH AN OLD LADY. I'M OUT.

AW, YOU GUYS SUCK! WHERE YOU ALL GOING?
COME BACK!
WE'RE GONNA GO BOB FOR APPLES, SINCE YOU ATE ALL THE HORS D'OEUVRES!
I CAN'T BELIEVE WE'RE DOING THIS KIDDIE SHIT. WHAT A STUPID HALLOWEEN!
OH, IT'S FUN TO DO AND YOU KNOW IT.
YEAH, LET THE CHICKS BOB, YOU KNOW?
Dude, I hope she never gets an apple.
I'd like to get some of *them* apples, though.
SHUBBB UBB!
I WONDER WHERE THOSE DAMN JESUS HEADS HAVE BEEN HIDING FOR THE LAST HALF-HOUR?
WHAT?!
ZOOB ZOOB

OH, NO! CLOVER, DON'T--!
ACK!

ACK! AAAACK!
GUYS!!! CLOVER'S GAGGING!

SHE FIT A WHOLE APPLE IN HER THROAT?!
YEAH! CLOVER, IF YOU SURVIVE THIS, I PROMISE TO MARRY YOU!
SOMEONE SHUT UP AND GIVE HER THE HINDLICK!
HEIMLICH, ASS MONSTER!

YOU FUCKERS! STOP CHOKING HER!
COME ON, CLOVER!
BLAAAGH!
Haw! That looks like Bleu's doing Clover doggy style!

AAAP! AAAP!
WHERE'S THE APPLE? I CAN'T FIND IT.
DAMN, I LOST THEM AGAIN!

JAYSUS, *wheeze* THAT DIDN'T FEEL LIKE AN APPLE!
IT FELT LIKE SOMETHING HARD WAS BEING JAMMED DOWN MY THROAT!

IF YOU ENJOYED THAT, I CAN MAKE IT HAPPEN FOR YOU AGAIN, AND AGAIN, AND AGAIN!

WHAT WAS THAT FOR?!
ALL RIGHT, I'M READY TO TELL MY STORY.

"IT WAS A DARK AND STORMY NIGHT...BUT BAD WEATHER SELDOM PHASES THE YOUNG, SO A VERY PARTICULAR PAIR OF TEENAGERS DROVE THEIR WAY THROUGH LIGHTNING AND UNRELENTING RAIN IN ORDER TO GO TO THE SOPHOMORE SOCK HOP WHEN SUDDENLY A TIRE BLEW OUT OR SOMETHING..."
WHAT THE FUCK WAS THAT?!
THE WHO "BORIS THE SPIDER"

SHIT, I THINK WE BLEW A TIRE!
GUESS THAT'S WHAT I GET FOR SWERVING TO HIT SQUIRRELS...

I'M SURE THERE'S NO HELP FOR MILES... heh-heh...
WAIT, DIDN'T WE SEE A CASTLE BACK THERE?
WHAT CASTLE? I SAW NO CASTLE.
I THINK THERE'S SOMETHING UNDER THE STEERING WHEEL YOU MIGHT WANT TO LOOK AT, THOUGH.

THE CASTLE WE JUST PASSED? IT'S KIND OF HARD TO MISS.
OH, ALL RIGHT. I'LL GO TO THE STUPID CASTLE. SIT TIGHT.
NO, I'M GOING TOO. YOU MIGHT SEE SOME OTHER HOTTIES AND FORGET ALL ABOUT ME.
YOU'RE RIGHT, YOU BETTER COME ALONG.

I DON'T KNOW ABOUT YOU, CHAD, BUT I'M NOT SINGING UNTIL WE HIT THE CASTLE.
YEAH, IT'LL MAKE THE TRIP GO A LOT FASTER.

KA-RAK
ENTER AT YOUR OWN RISK.

"SO THEY ARRIVED AT THE STUPID CASTLE AND A VERY, EXTREMELY, INCREDIBLY WEIRD GUY ANSWERED THE DOOR."
YESSSS???
SQUUUUUEEEEE

HELLO! MY NAME IS CHAD WALSH, AND THIS IS MY COMPLETELY NEUROTIC GIRLFRIEND, JANIE FINNEGAN!
'SUP, BABY? I'M MISH MASH.
H-HI.

YOU LOOK A LITTLE COLD-- HOW'S ABOUT YOU COME INSIDE AND I TOWEL YOU OFF *REEEEAL* NICE AND SLOW-LIKE?
I'M NOT THAT KIND OF GIRL!
TOWEL HER OFF? HELL, YOU CAN KEEP HER IF YOU LET ME USE YOUR PHONE!

KLA RAK

YOU'D BETTER *COME INSIDE.*
BUT WE'VE BARELY MET...
SHUT UP, DORK!

AAA! HOW'D WE END UP IN OUR UNDER-WEAR?
TOO BAD I DIDN'T WEAR ANY!
REALLY, I JUST WANT TO USE YOUR PHONE, THEN WE'LL LEAVE YOU TO YOUR CELEBRA-TION...!
THUMP THUMPA THUMPA
WE? I'M KEEPING THE NEUROTIC GIRL, REMEMBER? PHONE'S THIS WAY, KIDS.

Everybody's doing a brand new dance noooow come on baby, do the Locomotion!!
SOME SORTA ANNUAL FREAK CONVENTION, LTD.

HOLY MARY MOTHER CHRIST ALMIGHTY, THAT ISN'T THE RIGHT SONG!
IT'S NOT?

All I wanna do is zoom a zoom zoom zoom and a boom boom-- JUST SHAKE YO' RUMP!
NO, NO, NO!!!
One night in Bangkok makes a hard man humble--
NO, NO--LIKE THIS!
Well it's the pelvic thruuuust that really drives us in-saaa-yaay-yaay-yain!
Let's do the Time Warp agaaaaain!
HEY, WHAT ABOUT ME?
Well, I was running into the bathroom just to yak in the sink, when I missed the washbin and doused some guy in chowdery stink!

He cleaned hisself up while staring at my thighs, he had a JP200 and wicked black Levis!

He glared at me and demanded my change, that's the last time I'll puke on some dumb guy again!

I LIKE THIS STORY. I HAVEN'T BEEN BEAT UP OR TURNED INTO A WEREWOLF OR ANYTHING!

REALLY, WE JUST WANTED TO USE YOUR PHONE, YOU GOOFY BASTARDS!!!

AH! OHHH...

NOOO! IT'S HORRIBLE!!!

I'M JUST A SWEET TRANS-VESTITE!

We Love our Chris, yes we do!

AAAAAAAAAAAAAAAAAAAAAAAAAAAAAAAAAAAAAAA!!!!!!!!!!!!!!!!

NO MORE, NO MORE! LOOK, MONKEYBOY'S PASSED OUT!

BUT YOU HAVEN'T SEEN DR. FULUFFLUPHAGUS' INVENTION YET!
WHAT'S HIS INVENTION?

"HIS IDEAL MAN!"
GOLD
UMMM...

SQUEAL!
AW, GAAAD!

OH, DON'T BE SO HOMO-PHOBIC!
WE'RE NOT, WE'RE FREAKING OUT BECAUSE THOSE ARE THE LAST TWO GUYS WE'D WANNA SEE IN UNDERWEAR, LET ALONE LINGERIE!

YOU MEAN TO TELL ME YOU GUYS HAVE NEVER SEEN THE ROCKY HORROR PICTURE SHOW?
NOOOO...
TCH, VIRGINS.

WHAT? YOU SAID YOU WERE A VIRGIN, TOO!
I'M NOT A VIRGIN, DON'T PUT ME ON YOUR LOSER LIST.
I WASN'T TALKING ABOUT SEX, YOU MORON!
IT'S WHAT YOU CALL PEOPLE WHO HAVE NEVER SEEN THE MOVIE BEFORE--OH, NEVER MIND!

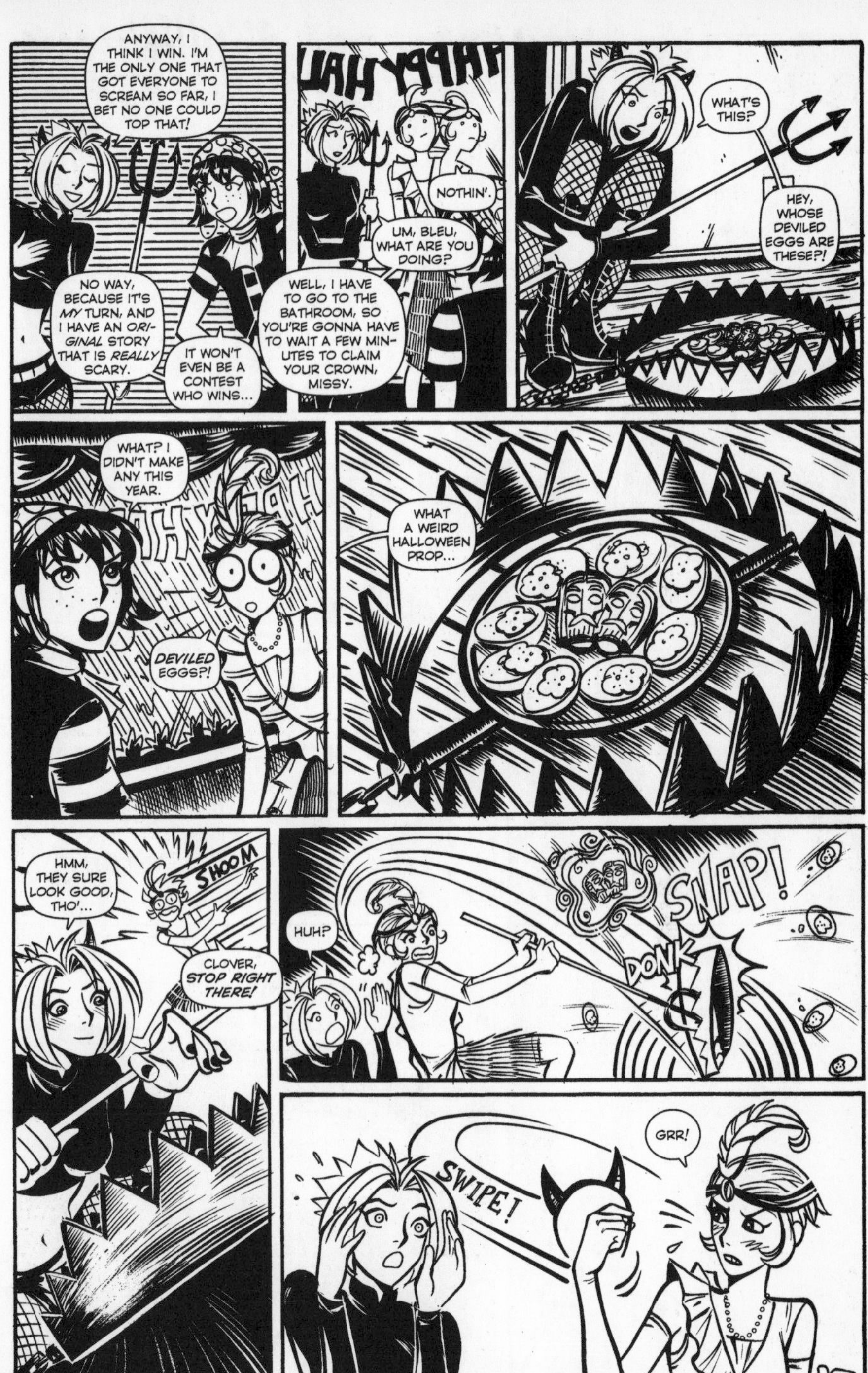
ANYWAY, I THINK I WIN. I'M THE ONLY ONE THAT GOT EVERYONE TO SCREAM SO FAR, I BET NO ONE COULD TOP THAT!
NO WAY, BECAUSE IT'S *MY* TURN, AND I HAVE AN *ORIGINAL* STORY THAT IS *REALLY* SCARY.
IT WON'T EVEN BE A CONTEST WHO WINS...
HAPPY HAL
NOTHIN'.
UM, BLEU, WHAT ARE YOU DOING?
WELL, I HAVE TO GO TO THE BATHROOM, SO YOU'RE GONNA HAVE TO WAIT A FEW MINUTES TO CLAIM YOUR CROWN, MISSY.
WHAT'S THIS?
HEY, WHOSE DEVILED EGGS ARE THESE?!
WHAT? I DIDN'T MAKE ANY THIS YEAR.
DEVILED EGGS?!
WHAT A WEIRD HALLOWEEN PROP...
HMM, THEY SURE LOOK GOOD, THO'...
SHOOM
CLOVER, *STOP RIGHT THERE!*
HUH?
SNAP!
DONK
GRR!
SWIPE!

ZOOP
SLAM!
?
LOOK, CLOVER'S NOT REALLY A DEVIL! IT'S HALLOWEEN, THESE ARE FAKE! SO STOP TRYING TO WHACK HER, OKAY?!?
ZOOP?
YES, REALLY!
ZOOP
IT'S ALL RIGHT, JUST STOP CAUSING TROUBLE TO-NIGHT, OKAY?
SIGH.
KNOCK KNOCK
WHAT, I TOLD YOU GUYS TO--
--NO!
TRICKS OR TREATS, BABY!
"Now allow me to intro-duce myself. My name is HUUUMPTY. Pronounced with an 'UMPTY..."
NO! OUT! OUT!
COME ON! YOU KNOW ME!
I once got busy in a Burger King bathroom! Doo woo-dooo woop!
GO AWAY!
BUT YOU LEFT A JACK-O'-LANTERN OUT FOR ME! YOU ASKED ME TO COME!
I DID NOT! NOW PISS OFF, I CAN'T HANDLE TWO--NO, THREE--SPIRITS IN ONE NIGHT!
FINE, BUT I'M NOT GONNA FORGET THIS! SEE IF I SHOW UP AGAIN WHEN YOU NEED ME!

WENCH!
GOD, THIS NIGHT!

ALRIGHT, I'M BACK. HERE'S YOUR HORNS, CLOVER.
T'ANKS, SPA.
IT'S ABOUT TIME!
UGH, I'M SICK OF THESE DUMB STORIES.

IT WAS ON A NIGHT JUST LIKE TONIGHT...
CLICK
WHRRRR
HEY, THE LIGHTS ARE BACK ON!
I'M SIIINGIN' IN THE RAIN! JUST SIIINGIN' IN THE RAIN--VIDDY WELL, LITTLE BROTHER! VIDDY WELL!
AH!
HEH-HEH!
!

YEAH! CLOCKWORK ORANGE IS ON!!!
HEY!!! GET BACK HERE!

SEE IF I EVER INVITE YOU GUYS TO ANOTHER PARTY!
-Snif-
AW, ERIN! FIX YOUR TV! THE RECEPTION IS ALL FUZZY!

HUH? WHAT ARE YOU TALKING ABOUT?

CHRIST, WHEN DID HE SHOW UP?
MAN, WHO CUT THE CHEESE?
'BOUT HALF AN HOUR AGO. SORRY, MAN. YOU SHOULDA BLOWN OUT THEM JACK-O'-LANTERNS, AFTER ALL.
SHIT, IT SHOULD BE WORKING!
THE RAMONES "HOWLING AT THE MOON (SHA-LA-LA)"
AW, MAAAAAAAN!
YAY!
HEY, ERIN--REMEMBER THAT STORY YOU WERE GONNA TELL US?
ZOOP ZOOP!
THERE IS...A HOUSE...IN FRES-BURGEEERR--THEY CALL IT THE RISING BUM!
LOVELY DEVILED EGGS, SIRS.
GOODNIGHT, LITTLE DROOGIES.

"Blue Belles"

A special cross-over with Paul Dini's *Jingle Belle*.

This page: Cover for the December 2002 Worlds of Westfield *catalogue, featuring the characters from Chynna's book* Scooter Girl.

This page: Chynna drew the cover to Paul Dini's Jingle Belle Winter Wingding.

Blue Belle's

WIFF SPECIAL FANKS TO LISSA READ & PAUL!

SOUNDTRACK BY FISHBONE & LORDS OF ACID! SEP 2000 ~A BLUE MONDAY · JINGLE BELLE JOINT~ BY CHYNNA CLUGSTON-MAJOR EDITED BY THE GRINCH IMSELF- JAMIE S. RICH

JESUS! GOOD WORK, MAN!
WELL, SCREW FOOD RIGHT NOW, LET'S GET TO THE PRESENTS!
VICTOR, ALAN, CLOVER, BLEU, PAUL...
WRAPPED IN A CEREAL BOX! FIGURES!
WOT THE HELL IS THIS?!
THEY'RE LICORICE UNDERWEAR! HAHAHA!
AND A NOTE! "CAN I EAT THEM OFF YOUR-
YACH!
HAHAHA!
WHAT'S THIS?! IT'S WEIRD!
IT'S A GOOD LUCK CHARM, Y'PRICK!
AW, MAN. I WAS HOPING FOR SOME NUDIE PHOTOS OF BETTY PAGE OR SOMETHING.
THWAK
Some Charm!
A DISK GUN! WOO!
I GAVE HIM THE "BUCKET O' FUN," FULLA TOYS AND SURE TO PLEASE DUMB BOYS!
LESSEE WHAT I GOT! ... SOAP. GEE, THANKS.
You can use it all in one place, too.
AW MAN! CHERRY FLAVORED VASE-MO-LINE, TURKEY BASTER, JELL-O PACKETS...
MWA HA HA
WHAT'S THIS? OH MY GOD! IT'S THE CAR TROUBLE 45 I'VE BEEN LOOKING FOR FOR YEARS! THANK YOU THANK YOU!
HEY, I DON'T REMEMBER YOU PUTTING THAT IN THERE!
OW!
HA!
BOP
OPEN YOURS, ALAN!
GREAT.
AREN'T I SEXY?
HAHAHA!
SNORT HA HA
BOP
GRR
GIMME THAT!
SWIPE!
TOSS
!
HAHA!
YOU SUCK!
TCH
YIIIIIIII!!
FWUMP
MORE PANELS THAN YOU CAN SHAKE A STICK AT!

JESUS, YOU O.K.?
BABE! BABE! BABE!
WHAT?! IN THE TREE?!!
ZOOM
WHAT?
...STARE MUCH?
THANK YOU, GOD! THANK YOU!!
SHOOM
UHH, ANY PARTICULAR REASON YOU WERE UP A TREE AT MIDNIGHT IN A GRAVEYARD WEARING AN ELF COSTUME ON CHRISTMAS EVE?
YEAH, ACTUALLY... IT HAS A LOT TO DO WITH THE FACT THAT I HAVE TO HELP MY CHUNKY DAD DELIVER GIFTS ALL DAMN NIGHT THIS TIME EVERY YEAR!
YOU'RE SAYIN' YOU'RE SANTA CLAUSE'S DAUGHTER?
HOY, WE'VE GOT A FRIGGIN' COMEDIAN HERE!
GOT A PROBLEM, IRISH?!
WOT, WANT TO DANCE, NANOOK?
BABES, BABES! NO NEED FOR FIGHTS, THIS IS THE SEASON OF GIVING!
YEAH, GIMME SOMMA THAT!
I HEARD SOMETHING ABOUT EGG NOG... GOT ENOUGH FOR ONE MORE?
YEAH!!
SHLURP
THIS EGGNOG IS WEAK! GIMME THAT!
SWIPE!
REMIND ME NEVER TO WASH THAT JUG AGAIN!
YOU NEED TO BE SCHOOLED BY THE MASTER OF HOLIDAY DRINKS...
THIS IS HOW YOU DO IT, BOYS.
XX NOG
SHAKA SHAKA
SHAKA
RUN THAT BY US AGAIN?
PLEASE?

AND SO THE GOOD CHILDREN FEASTED...
YARF
YARM
SO, WHAT'S YOUR NAME, BEAUTIFUL?
M'NAME'S JINGLE BELLE.
SHOULD BE "JIGGLE BUTT"!
SHH DUDE! NO FIGHTS TONIGHT!
NO, GORGEOUS. YOUR REAL NAME.
YEAH, NOT YOUR STRIPPER ALIAS!
STRIPPER ALIAS! I'M BETTER THAN ANY DAMN STRIPPER!
BETTER THAN A STRIPPER? YOU'VE DONE STUFF LIKE THAT BEFORE?
SURE, ESKIMO BOYS LIKE KINKY CHICKS, NOT ALL THAT GOODY-GOODY NOSE KISSIN' SHTUFF.
I BET YOU'RE TOO SHY TO PROVE IT.
WHAT!
YEAH... SHE DOESN'T LOOK LIKE THE TYPE TO LIVE UP TO ALL HER BIG TALK!
FINE! HERE, MUSHROOM HEAD. SLAP THIS ON AND WE'LL SEE IF I'M SHY!
HA HA
LORDS OF ACID*
* THE MOST WONDERFUL GIRL
COME ON!
I'M @!!$& ING BEAUTIFUL...
RIP
I'M THE GREATEST THING
I'VE EVER SEEN!
GOD I LOVE MYSELF...
Oh, my god...
SO THIS IS CHRISTMAS!
GO! GO!
I'M SEXY...
I'M GORGEOUS
HEY, LOOK!
WE ARE! AMAZING, AREN'T THEY!
YES! ELF KNOCKERS!
JINGLE BELLE!
IT'S REALLY SANTA!
DAD!?! HOW'D YOU FIND ME?!?
I WAS WAY AHEAD OF YOU THIS YEAR, I PUT A TRACKING DEVICE IN YOUR NEW SNOWBOOTS! YOU ARE GROUNDED YOUNG LADY, FOR THE NEXT TEN YEARS!!!
GOD! YOU'RE SO MEAN!
INTO THE SLEIGH JINGLE... AND COVER YOURSELF!
I KNEW SHE WASN'T LYIN'!
AND SO ENDED THE MOST MEMORABLE CHRISTMAS EVE EVER FOR THE STRANGE KIDS FROM JEFFERSON HIGH SCHOOL. THEY ENJOYED INNUMERABLE EXPENSIVE GIFTS FROM AN ANONYMOUS PARTY FOR MANY, MANY YEARS TO COME AFTERWARD... SEEMINGLY DUE TO A PROMISE THEY MADE TO KEEP SOME DELICATE INFORMATION UNDER WRAPS... THE END!
UH, MERRY X-MAS!
WOAH.
LATER, YULE BABE!
I LOVE YOOOOOU!

FROM:
-03

FASHION FAIR MALL, DECEMBER 26th.
I TOTALLY RETURNED THAT GROSS SWEATER MY DAD BOUGHT ME WITH THE SNOWFLAKES AND REINDEER ON IT.
WHAT WAS HE THINKING?
I GOT A COUPLE CDs AND A ROBERT SMITH POSTER WITH THE DOUGH FROM MY GRANDMA.
I GOT THAT PICTURE JINGLE BELLE GAVE ME FRAMED UP!
WHAT? WHEN DID SHE GIVE YOU A PICTURE? BASTARD!
ORANGE JULIUS
DEPECHE MODE - HAPPIEST GIRL
IT WAS IN MY STOCKING YESTERDAY MORNING! I'M GONNA PUT IT RIGHT NEXT TO MY BED-SO THAT I HAVE HOT, SEX-FILLED DREAMS EVERY NIGHT... GUARANTEED!
THAT'S A SMART MOVE. THE PICTURE WILL LAST LONGER WITHOUT POOLS OF SPOO GUMMIN' IT UP.
WHAT ABOUT YOU, CLOVER? WHAT'D YOU GET?
SOMETHING THAT FITS MY MOOD AND THE OCCASION.
OCCASION? WHAT OCCASION?
WHAT, IS IT "I'M-A-RAGING-BITCH BECAUSE-I-DIDN'T GET-THE-PRESENTS I-WANTED-DAY?"
NOT QUITE.
PUM
SHOULD HAVE SEEN THAT COMING... IT'S...
HA HA HA!!! MODED!
...BOXING DAY!
(PROPS TO JON FOR THE HOLIDAY SUGGESTION)

"Lovecats"

MOZ

VALENTINE'S DAY.
HAIRCUT 100, "LOVE PLUS ONE"
...CLEARLY CYNICAL, BUT PERHAPS NOT WITHOUT REASON.
WHAT I WANT YOU TO DO IS WRITE AN ESSAY ON WHAT YOU THINK THE WRITER MEANS. DON'T SNIVEL, YOU HAVE FORTY-FIVE MINUTES TO FINISH IT!
"The worst of having a romance of any kind is that it leaves one so unromantic."
-Oscar Wilde (The Picture of Dorian Gray)
PRETTY SELF-EXPLANATORY, ISN'T IT?

DUDE, I CAN'T BELIEVE WE HAD DETENTION ALL THROUGH LUNCH ON TODAY OF ALL DAYS. HOW STUPID!
YEAH, Y'MIGHT HAVE GOTTEN THAT HUGE BOUQUET OF ROSES AND BALLOONS WAITING FOR YOU AT THE TREE AND THE SKY-WRITTEN PROPOSAL FROM MR. BISHOP HAD WE NOT BEEN TOSSED INTO A CUBICLE ALL HOUR.
AW, SHUDDUP. CAN I BORROW SOME PAPER?

THANKS. AT LEAST THERE'S THE DANCE TONIGHT. DANCES ALWAYS MAKE UP FOR EVERYTHING. I'LL FEEL MUCH BETTER AFTER I GET MY GROOVE ON.
HAVE FUN, THEN.

WHAT? YOU AREN'T GOING?! WHY???
IT'S A BLOODY VALENTINE'S DANCE! IT'S A TERRIBLE HOLIDAY, I DON'T LIKE IT, ALL THEY'RE GOING TO PLAY ARE SLOW SONGS, EVERYONE DROOLING ALL OVER EACH OTHER...
AND I THINK IF I HEAR "LOVE HURTS" ONE MORE TIME I'M GOING TO GO FOKIN' MENTAL!
I CAN'T GO, IT'S UNHEALTHY.

"UNHEALTHY"?
FOR EVERYONE ELSE. I'LL HAVE TO BEAT THE LIFE OUT OF EVERYBODY THERE! I TOLD YOU DAYS AGO I WASN'T GOING.
AW, COME ON! THE WHOLE CREW WILL BE THERE!
WELL, EXCEPT VICTOR, COS SALLY DIDN'T WANT TO GO WITH HIM.
SALLY. YEAH.

CAN YOU BELIEVE HE ASKED HER? WHAT'S HE SMOKING?
WHAT VICTOR WAS SMOKING!
TO AVOID BEING DATELESS AT THIS PARTICULAR VALENTINE'S DAY DANCE, VICTOR GOMEZ DECIDES TO TAKE A GAMBLE AND WRITE A CHEESY LOVE LETTER TO DUMP IN EITHER BLEU, ERIN, OR CLOVER'S LOCKER.
UKIBE
COVERED IN "BLUE MONDAY: CONTAGEOUSLY YOURS", AVAILABLE IN THE KIDS ARE ALRIGHT! -- NOT-THE-EDITOR
THE FIRST TWO ALREADY HAVING DATES, VICTOR DECIDED TO GIVE THE LETTER TO CLOVER AND WAIT FOR HER EXCITED RESPONSE TO COME IN A GUSH OF JOYFUL TEARS.
OF COURSE SHE'D BE HAPPY TO GO, WHY WOULDN'T SHE?
Fantasy!
MY LIFE IS NOW COMPLETE! THANK YOU, GOD!
PLEASE TRY TO CONTROL YOURSELF, CLOVER.
SHOOM!
Reality!
WOT THE FOK IS THIS?
RECOGNIZING THE FACT THAT IT WAS INTENDED TO WOO WHOEVER SHOULD READ IT FIRST (BEING SO CLICHE, AND HER NAME WASN'T EVEN ON THE LETTER)...
MASH MASH MASH
...CLOVER SHOVED THE DUMB NOTE INTO HER NEIGHBOUR SALLY'S LOCKER, GIVING VICTOR A SPECIAL "FEK AFF, YA BASTARD" FROM THE ONE AND ONLY.
VICTOR, HOWEVER, THINKS HE MESSED UP AND DOESN'T REALIZE HE REALLY DID GIVE IT TO CLOVER AND NOT SALLY... AND AS A RESULT LOSES ALL NERVE TO ASK CLOVER TO THE DANCE.
NO. NO FOKIN' WAY.
SECRETLY, THE UNFORTUNATE DUO BOTH WANT TO GO REALLY BADLY. BUT THEY WON'T TELL ANYONE.

BUT, CLOVER, I WON'T BE SLOBBERING ON MY FRIEND FROM MY OLD SCHOOL, I TOLD YOU IT'S NOT LIKE THAT. WE HAVEN'T HUNG OUT SINCE BEFORE I TRANSFERRED FROM ROOSEVELT LAST YEAR, AND I WANT YOU TO MEET HIM, HE'S FUNNY AS HELL! YOU GOTTA COME!
NO. FORGET IT. I DON'T WANT TO GO.
THE KIN
BODDINGTON
WHAT DO YOU MEAN YOU DON'T WANT TO GO?
JUST WHAT I SAID.
WHY, BECAUSE CLOVER MADE FUN OF YOU ASKING SALLY YESTERDAY?
I DIDN ASK SALL DO SHIT! T IRISH TART MAKING THIN UP JUST TO F WITH ME!
I DIDN'T KNOW YOU HAD A THING FOR SALLY.
I'D SOONER CASTRATE MYSELF THAN ASK HER OUT.
SHE RUNS TO EVERY CLASS STARING AT HER FEET AND FALLING IN DITCHES!
SHE PICKS HER NOSE WITH HER NUMBER-TWO PENCIL AND THEN CHEWS ON THE ERASER!
DUDE, I KNOW WHAT YOU WERE UP TO. YOU CAN'T HIDE THAT SHIT FROM ME.
YOU WERE WRITING CLOVER A LOVE LETTER! HER LOCKER IS RIGHT NEXT TO SALLY'S.
I WAS NOT.
OH? I KNOW YOU *LIKE* HER.
IT'S PLAIN AS DAY, YOU KNOW.
YEAH? WELL, I LIKE ANYTHING WITH TITS AND A PAIR OF DOCS.
SO WHAT'S THE BIG DEAL? WHY DON'T YOU JUST ASK HER OUT?
...OR CAN'T YOU MAKE UP YOUR MIND WHO YOU *REALLY* LIKE?
...
YOU SHOULD FIGURE IT OUT, GENIUS... BEFORE THEY *ALL* GET TAKEN AND YOU'RE STUCK WITH YOUR RIGHT HAND.
FUCK OFF.
I USE MY LEFT.
ECHO AND THE BUNNYMEN "LIPS LIKE SUGAR"

LOVE IS A BURNIN' THAAAANG... AND IT MAKES A FIREY RAAANG...
HEY, VICTOR.
I HEAR CLOVER'S NOT GOING TO THE DANCE BECAUSE SHE DOESN'T HAVE A DATE. WHY DON'T YOU TWO GO TOGETHER?
!
I FELL INTO A BURNIN' RING-A FIIIIRE!
SOK
YOU ASSHOLE! SHUT UP!!!
I AIN'T GOIN' TO THE FOKIN' DANCE COS I DON'T WANT TO GO TO THE FOKIN' DANCE, NOT FOR LACK OF A DATE. SO PISS OFF, WALSH.
I WENT DOWN, DOWN, DOWN, AND THE FLAMES WENT HIGHAAAA--
CLOVER, YOU CAN'T MISS THIS ONE. I'M JUST GOING TO HAVE TO GET YOU IN THE MOOD TO GO.
HOW'S THAT?
BY SINGING!
TRUUUE LOOOOVE... YOU'RE THE ONE I'M DREAMING OF, YOUR HEART FITS ME LIKE A GLOOOOVE, SOMETHIN' SOMETHIN', TRUE BLUE, BABY, I LOVE YOU!
THAT IS NOT GOING TO WORK.
WRONG SONG, ISN'T IT?
HOW ABOUT, HOWEVER FAR AWAAY, I WILL ALWAYS LOVE YOU... HOW-EVER LONG I STAY, I WILL ALWAYS LOVE YOUUU... WHATEVER WORDS I SAY I WILL ALWAYS LOVE YOU--
NO!
OKAY, OKAY. I'M SORRY. I'LL SHUT UP.
SHUT UP!

RELAX, BABEH, NOW WE'RE ALL ALOOONE!
OW!

LOVE BITES!
LOVE BLEEDS!
IT'S BRINGIN' ME TO MAH KNEES...!
OOOH!
SHUT OP, YA DAFT LITTLE BRAT!
DRAG

AW, CLOVER, IT WON'T BE THE SAME IF YOU DON'T COME THIS YEAR.
DON'T YOU REMEMBER LAST VALENTINE'S DAY?
YEAH, IT WAS SHITE.
SQUEEZE
HOW CAN YOU SAY THAT?
I MET *YOU* AT THAT DANCE LAST YEAR.
THAT'S WHAT I'M TALKING ABOUT.
HA-HA. VERY FUNNY, YOU BITCH.
I REMEMBER THAT DAY. HOW DID YOU GUYS MEET AGAIN?

I'D ONLY BEEN AT JEFFERSON FOR ABOUT A WEEK, AND ERIN WAS THE ONLY PERSON I KNEW.
SOCIAL DISTORTION "BAD LUCK"
SHE TOLD ME I SHOULD GO TO THE DANCE, COZ SHE'D BE THERE AND I COULD MEET SOME OTHER KIDS AND HAVE A GOOD TIME.
TONIGHT 8 DANCE!
8PM
OF COURSE, I GOT THERE BEFORE SHE DID, AND I STILL DIDN'T KNOW ANYONE ELSE.
I FELT LIKE THE BIGGEST IDIOT (DON'T YOU DARE SAY ANYTHING, ALAN).
I WAS DESPERATE TO FIND SOMEONE, ANYBODY I THOUGHT LOOKED INTERESTING ENOUGH TO TRY TO BEFRIEND.
YA-HOO
HEE-HAW
HMM, HE'S KINDA CUTE.
SIGH HAS A GIRL-FRIEND. BIG SURPRISE.
HUH?
A PUNK! THANK GOD...
HEH.
HAVE YOU EVER SEEN SO MANY SHIT-KICKERS IN YOUR LIFE?
ISN'T THAT ALL THERE IS IN AMERICA?

UHHH... NO, NOT REALLY...
HMPH.
I GUESS YOU'D GET THAT IDEA, GOING TO A SCHOOL IN THE FOOTHILLS... TO A DANCE WHERE ALL THEY PLAY IS DEF LEPPARD, NAZARETH, AND COUNTRY.
>GRUNT<
IF ONLY THEY'D PLAY SOME CURE AND DEPECHE MODE...
ROMANTIC *SHITE.*
WELL, YOU CAN'T DANCE TO THE DEAD KENNEDYS!
ALL YA CAN DO IS PULL TAFFY TO THE CURE!
YOU CAN DANCE TO THE CURE.
YOU CAN'T.
CAN.
CAN'T.
ROXY MUSIC "LOVE IS THE DRUG"
I LOVE DANCES. DON'T YOU LOVE DANCES?
LOVE 'EM.
I'D LIKE THEM BETTER IF THERE WAS GOOD MUSIC PLAYING.
I REQUESTED SOME STUFF, BUT I BET THEY'RE TOO LAME TO PLAY IT.
IF THEY PLAYED A GOOD SONG, I'D TOTALLY ASK A CHICK TO DANCE.
YEAH? WHICH ONE, DUDE?

HMM... WHO WOULD BE THE LUCKY LADY?
LUCKY LAYDEH, LUCKY LAYDEH...

OH, SHIT! SHE'S HERE!
WHO?

THAT ONE, THE ONE I ALWAYS SEE WALKING PAST DRIVER'S ED! THE PUNK CHICK THAT BEAT UP THAT DICK WESLEY STEIN-HOSER! SHE SAID "HI" TO ME ONCE!
OH, THAT'S THE GIRL THAT TURNED AROUND AND SAID "HI" TO YOU BECAUSE YOU KEPT STARING AT HER EVERY TIME SHE PASSED BY AND YOU DIDN'T SAY ANYTHING BACK BECAUSE YOU WERE SO FREAKED OUT SHE TALKED TO YOU?
THAT ONE?

I DON'T KNOW WHERE YOU HEARD *THAT*, BUT...
WHO'S THAT WITH HER?
MOZ

I DUNNO, BUT SHE'S PRETTY CUTE TOO. MAN!
TARGETS ACQUIRED!

WHAT'S YOUR SHIRT SAY? "STAY SICK." HOLY SHIT, YOU LISTEN TO THE CRAMPS?!
YOU'RE THE ONLY ONE AT THIS SCHOOL THAT I BET LIKES THEM BESIDES ME!
WHAT, YOU LIKE THEM TOO?
YOU?

I *LOVE* THE CRAMPS.
"CREATURE FROM THE BLACK LEATHER LAGOON" IS MY FAVORITE SONG OF THEIRS.
PLUS, "SURFIN' DEAD," 'CAUSE IT WAS IN *RETURN OF THE LIVING DEAD*, MY FAVORITE ZOMBIE MOVIE.
GOOD FILM.

HEY, YOUR ACCENT...
WOT ABOUT IT?
WELL, YOU'RE IRISH, AREN'T YOU?
CHRIST, SOMEONE GOT IT RIGHT. ALL THESE KNOBHEADS HAVE BEEN CALLING ME ENGLISH THE WHOLE TIME, IT'S DRIVING ME MAD.
WELL, I KNOW THE DIFFERENCE, ANYWAY. SO, WHAT'S YOUR STORY?
WHAT D'YOU MEAN?
YOU DON'T WANT TO BE HERE, SO WHY ARE YOU?
EH. ME DA.
HE MADE MY BROTHER TAKE ME SO I'D MAKE SOME FRIENDS.
HE SAID I'M TOO ANTI-SOCIAL, APPARENTLY. CAN YOU BLAME ME?
ANYWAY, THAT'S ME BROTHER AND HIS SLAG OVER THERE.
GRR...
VANDALS
SHOULDA GUESSED.
HEY, LOOK, THAT ENGLISH DYKE GOT HERSELF A GIRLFRIEND! NICE HAIR, BLUEBERRY!
TONE LOC
GO FUCK YOURSELF, OR I'LL KICK THE PISS OUT OF YOU AND YOUR BOYFRIENDS AGAIN!
OOOH! I'M SO SCARED.
HOW MANY EPISODES OF "MATLOCK" DID YOU WATCH BEFORE YOU WERE ABLE TO MEMORIZE THAT LINE? GO HOME.
BITCH...
NOTICE HE HAD TO HAVE THE WHOLE FOOTBALL TEAM SITTING BEHIND HIM IN ORDER TO SAY THAT WITHOUT PEEING HIS PANTS.
WELL, I'M REALLY THIRSTY. WANT TO GET SOME PUNCH?
SURE.
TO HELL WITH PERSPECTIVE! ...AT LEAST FOR THIS PANEL!

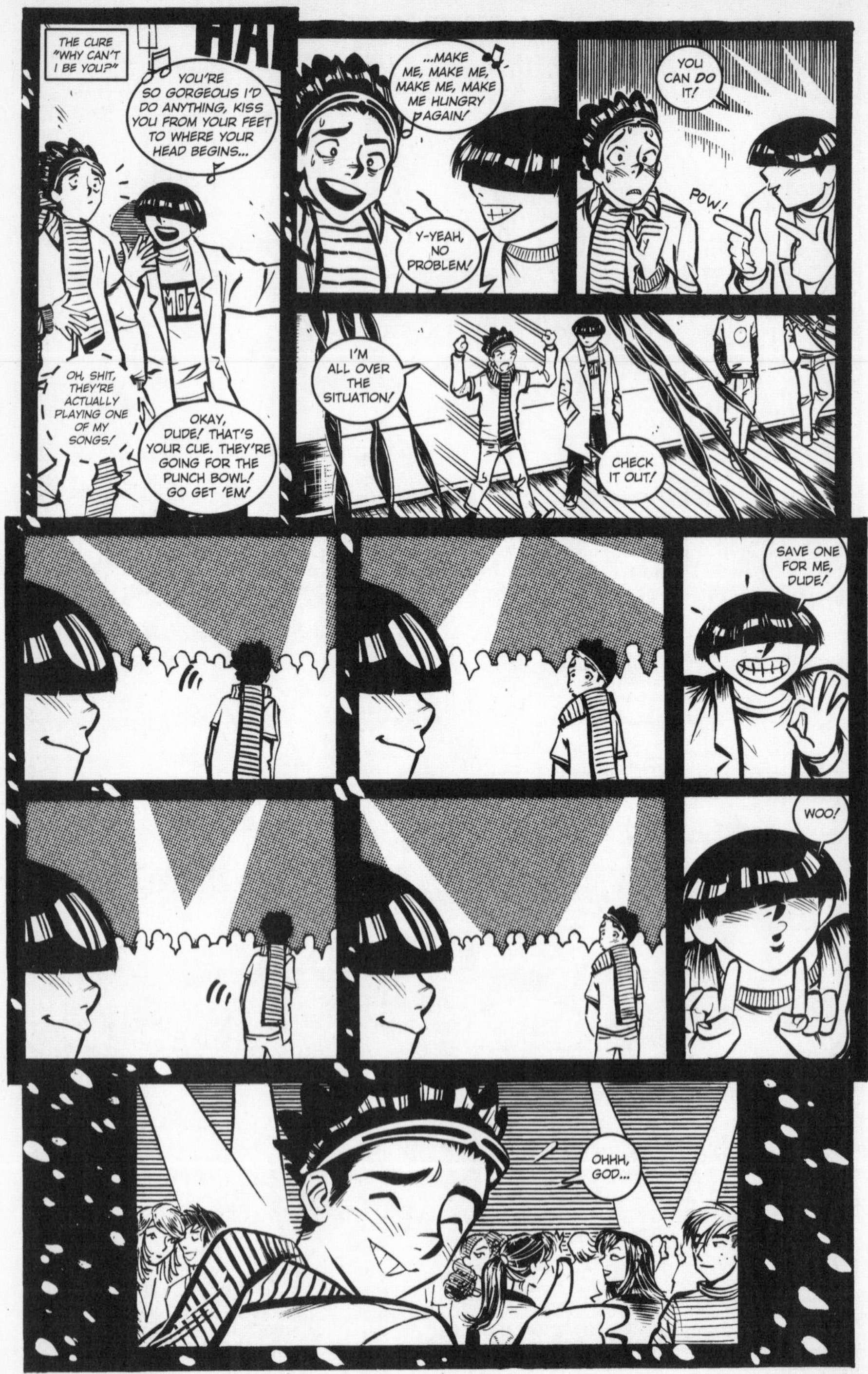
THE CURE "WHY CAN'T I BE YOU?"
YOU'RE SO GORGEOUS I'D DO ANYTHING, KISS YOU FROM WHERE YOUR FEET TO WHERE YOUR HEAD BEGINS...
OH, SHIT, THEY'RE ACTUALLY PLAYING ONE OF MY SONGS!
OKAY, DUDE! THAT'S YOUR CUE. THEY'RE GOING FOR THE PUNCH BOWL! GO GET 'EM!
...MAKE ME, MAKE ME, MAKE ME, MAKE ME HUNGRY AGAIN!
Y-YEAH, NO PROBLEM!
YOU CAN DO IT!
POW!
I'M ALL OVER THE SITUATION!
CHECK IT OUT!
SAVE ONE FOR ME, DUDE!
WOO!
OHHH, GOD...

SLOP
SEE? YOU CAN DANCE TO THIS SONG!

SHIT, I SPILLED SOME.
CAN YOU POUR ME ANOTHER?

I KNOW YOU.
UHH...

NICE GLASSES. I HAVE A PAIR, TOO.

YOU'RE THAT KID THAT BUGS OUT YOUR EYES WHEN PEOPLE TALK TO YOU.

ERR...
WANT SOME PUNCH?

'SOKAY, I'LL GET IT--

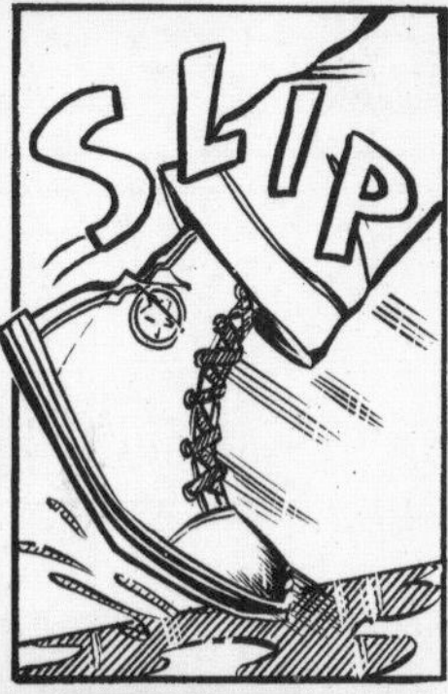
SLIP

BAM
AGH!!

AH, CHRIST!

OH, MAN, I'M SORRY!

I REALLY DIDN'T MEAN TO, HERE'S SOME NAPKINS--

SLIP!
SPANNER!

IF YOU DIDN'T KNOW EACH OTHER BEFORE, I'D SAY YOU KNOW EACH OTHER NOW.
IS THAT LEGAL IN PUBLIC?
SORRY! I'M SORRY!
I *HOPE* FOR YOUR SAKE THAT'S A PENCIL!
A SIMPLE *"HELLO"* WOULD HAVE DONE FINE, Y'KNOW!

HA HA HA HA HA HA HA OH GAAAD
ZOOM
SHUT UP, QUIT LAUGHING! COME ON!

SPIRIT
DO ALL THE BOYS IN THIS SCHOOL ASSAULT GIRLS AT PUNCH BOWLS, OR IS IT JUST THE QUIET ONES?
FOKIN' HELL, MY SHIRT.

WHAT ARE WE DOING?
WE'RE GETTING INTO THE LOCKER ROOM SO I CAN GET HER A REPLACEMENT FOR HER SHIRT.
MOZ

YOU THINK SHE WANTS YOUR STINKY SHIRT TO WEAR?
IT'S BETTER THAN A PUNCH-DRENCHED T-SHIRT, ISN'T IT?

NOT ACCORDING TO SMELL IT ISN'T.
I GOTTA TRY TO MAKE IT UP TO HER, OTHERWISE SHE'S GONNA HATE ME FOREVER.

WOULDN'T BLAME HER, THE WAY YOU ATTACKED HER, YOU RAPIST. HOW WAS YOUR FIRST TIME, ANYWAY? IT MUST HAVE BEEN WEIRD WITH ALL THOSE KIDS WATCHING.
the Cure

OH, GOD! NOW I'LL NEVER HAVE A CHANCE WITH HER!

SOB

WHEEW.

THE
PS

HI, BLEU. I SEE YOU'VE MET, AH...
CLOVER.
SNAP SNAP

RIIIGHT, CLOVER.
COME ON, BLEU, I WANT TO INTRODUCE YOU TO SOME PEOPLE...
TUG
WELL, I WAS JUST IN THE MIDDLE OF TALKING TO CLOVER.
I'LL BE RIGHT OVER IN A SEC, OKAY?

I GUESS. SEE YA IN A FEW MINUTES THEN.

THAT WAS ODD. SHE TRYING TO OWN YOU ALREADY?
WHAT DO YOU MEAN?
OH, NEVER MIND--
--HERE COMES MY BROTHER.

HOY, CLOVER. NICE SHIRT.
I'M GOING TO TAKE JENNY TO, UH, GET SOME ICE CREAM.
YOU MIND WAITING FOR US IN FRONT OF THE SCHOOL AFTER THE DANCE?
GO BADGERS
RAH
DO I HAVE A CHOICE?
VANDALS
NOT REALLY.

BRR!
HOW LONG IS IT GOING TO TAKE YOU TO "GET SOME ICE CREAM," THEN?

BEHEMOUTH
I DUNNO, A FEW HOURS.
PPPFT, A FEW SECONDS YOU MEAN.
VANDA
YOU REALIZE THERE'S SNOW OUTSIDE?
SO?

HEY, YOU KNOW, I'M SPENDING THE NIGHT AT ERIN'S HOUSE.
MAYBE SHE WOULDN'T MIND IF YOU CAME OVER, TOO. IT'D BE COOL.
BEATS THE SHIT OUT OF STANDING IN THE SNOW WAITING FOR YOUR BROTHER TO GET OFF-- ER, I MEAN...
YEAH, WHY DON'T YOU DO THAT?

I'LL JUST, UH, GO SEE WHAT ERIN THINKS.
YEAH.
RIGHT.

OKAY, LET'S GO GIVE HER THE SHIRT.
JUST PROMISE NOT TO FALL ON TOP OF HER AGAIN.
SHE MIGHT PRESS CHARGES THIS TIME.

UH, CLOVER?
WOT?
OH, IT'S YOU. FOKIN' FRED ASTAIRE.
DON'T COME ANY CLOSER IF THAT'S PUNCH IN YOUR HAND.

NO, I, UH, BROUGHT YOU A SHIRT, TO, Y'KNOW, WEAR, COS I MESSED UP THE ONE YOU HAVE ON. SORRY ABOUT THAT.
SORRY FOR WHAT?
MY TITS ARE PERMANENTLY FLAVORED LIKE TROPICAL PUNCH. IT'S JUST WHAT I ALWAYS WANTED. NO MAN CAN RESIST ME NOW.

HEH...
I'LL TAKE THE SHIRT, THANKS.

WHOO, STINKS, DON'T IT?
SORRY...
...
the Cure

IT'S ALL RIGHT, IT'S ONLY FROM SWEAT.
NOT AS IF HE WIPED HIS ARSE WITH IT.

SNIFF.
OR DID YA?

ERIN SAID IT WAS COOL.
GREAT. I'LL PICK YOU UP HERE TOMORROW AROUND NOON THEN.
SEE YA.
WELL, OKAY, I SUPPOSE.
HEY.
HEY.
HEY.
WHAT HAPPENED TO YOUR SHIRT, ANYWAY, CLOVER?
THAT GUY.
VICTOR DID THAT TO YOU?
OH, YEAH... WELL, HE'S PRETTY CLUMSY SOMETIMES.
HI, VICTOR. HI, MONKEYBOY. WHAT'S UP?
HI, ERIN.
SO IT HAS A NAME, DOES IT?
YEAH, VICTOR'S COOL. WE HAVE A CLASS TOGETHER. HE'S PRETTY FUNNY.
SHOULD BE. DRESSES LIKE A CLOWN.
DEVO!
HA HA HOH HOH HEE HEE
WHO'S THAT? DO YOU KNOW HIM?
OH, HIM?
...YEAH. THAT'S ALAN. I'VE TALKED TO HIM A FEW TIMES. HE HANGS OUT WITH MY NEIGHBOUR.
HE LIKES TO ARGUE A LOT.
THAT'S HIS GIRLFRIEND?
YEAH, A REAL BITCH, TOO. TOO BAD HE'S TAKEN, HUH?
WHAT?
NO, I MEAN, I JUST THOUGHT HE LOOKED KINDA INTERESTING IS ALL.

HEY, YOU GUYS WANT TO TAKE OFF AND HEAD OVER TO MY HOUSE? IT'S NOT FAR AWAY.
SURE, THIS DANCE IS GETTING WORSE BY THE MINUTE ANYWAY.
LEMME GO CHANGE MY SHIRT.
DUDE, ERIN LIVES REALLY CLOSE TO ME. SHE WALKS ALMOST THE SAME ROUTE AS I DO.
YEAH, AND...?
...OOOOH!
COME ON, LET'S WAIT OUTSIDE AND THEN FOLLOW 'EM.
DO YOU HAVE TO BE SUCH A HOLE RIGHT NOW?
JUST SHUT UP ABOUT IT!
GYM
FINE, I'M OUT OF HERE! FIND YOUR OWN WAY HOME!
STARE
STARE
FINE! PISS OFF THEN, STARFISH!

STARFISH?
HEE-HEE, SHE JUST LAYS THERE SPREAD EAGLE AND LETS HIM DO ALL THE WORK! STARFISH.
>SNORT<
RATHER WALK THAN HAVE TO KISS THAT MOUSTACHE OF YOURS AGAIN, ANYWAY.
HEY, CHRIS. GOT A SMOKE?
YEAH, HERE.
MOZ
THANKS.
LATER, GUYS.
Kiss Me Kiss Me Kiss Me
THANKS FOR THE SHIRT, SMOOTH OPERATOR.
BYE!
LAAAAATER...
...
UHHH, WELL, WE SHOULD GET GOING. CURFEW AND ALL THAT.
YEAH. LATER.
V-DAY DANCE TONIGHT 8:00pm

I WAS PASSING ERIN'S PLACE ON MY WAY HOME AND SAW HER LIGHT ON, SO I WENT UP TO THE FRONT DOOR--
THE FRONT DOOR? MORE LIKE YOU TRIPPED OVER THOSE TWO IDIOTS 'CAUSE THEY WERE ALREADY IN YOUR USUAL PEEPING BUSH.
YOU GUYS MADE SO MUCH NOISE, MY DEAD GRANDMOTHER COULD HAVE HEARD YOU.
I DON'T REMEMBER THAT.
YEAH, ME NEITHER.
THE
YEAH, AND THEN YOU INVITED THE PERVERTS IN AND WE ENDED UP PLAYING MONOPOLY AND LISTENING TO RECORDS ALL NIGHT...
...OR AT LEAST UNTIL THREE IN THE MORNING WHEN YOUR PARENTS KICKED THE GUYS OUT. THAT WAS A BLAST!
YEAH, THE DANCE SUCKED, BUT AFTERWARDS WAS TOTALLY GREAT.
UH-HUH, COS MONOPOLY IS JUST A LAUGH RIOT.
NO, IT WAS A WICKED GOOD TIME!
CÉ A BHÍ AG CAINT LEAT? *
YOU WERE, BITCH! COME ON. YOU KNOW YOU WANT TO GO!
* WHO WAS TALKING TO YOU?
SEE YOU TOMORROW.

IS IT TOO MUCH TO ASK TO NOT BE INSULTED FOR ONCE?
HOW COULD HE THINK I'D BE SO DAFT?
ANYBODY ACCEPTING THAT LETTER AS THE TRUTH WOULD HAVE TO BE AN IDIOT. I WISH I COULD BASH HIS STUPID HEAD IN!
SIGH
DON'T KNOW WHY I'VE BEEN FEELING SO MUSHY, ANYWAY. THAT'S BLEU'S DEPARTMENT... IT'S NOT ME.
BEEN WATCHING TOO MANY MOVIES, I THINK.
MUST BE BORED, I SUPPOSE.
SKASH!
SIGH
WHEN SMASHING STUFF DOESN'T MAKE ME LAUGH, SOMETHING'S DEFINITELY OFF-KILTER.

LATER, BACK AT ERIN'S HOUSE...
TMBG
STILL SUCK
RINGGG
HELLO?
DUDE! NATHAN ISN'T COMING NOW, AND CLOVER ISN'T GOING, OR VICTOR...
AIEEE!!
AND BOTH OF MY DATES HAVE BEEN GROUNDED!
NO WAY!
YEAH, THEIR PSYCHO MOM ATTACKS AGAIN.
SHE THINKS I DO COKE OR SOME-THING BECAUSE I HANG OUT WITH A "BLUE-HAIRED GIRL."
WELL, WE HAVE TO GO TOGETHER THEN.
AND WE HAVE TO TRY TO GET CLOVER AND VICTOR TO COME, TOO.
YEP.
YOU GET YOUR STUFF AND COME OVER SO WE CAN GET READY FOR THE DANCE, AND I'LL CALL THEM WHILE YOU'RE ON YOUR WAY.
ACE! OKAY, BYE!

HEY, WATTS. NOTHING VENTURED, NOTHING GAINED, RIGHT?
KEITH, ONCE A FOOL, ALWAYS A FOOL, RIGHT?
television
>GRUNT<
I GOTTA GET OUT OF HERE. I AM NOT STAYING HOME ON VALENTINE'S DAY.
I'D NEVER HEAR THE END OF IT FROM THOSE USELESS BROTHERS OF MINE, AND THAT'D MAKE ME HAVE TO KILL 'EM.
RRIIING!
VWIP!
I GOT IT!
HELLO?!?
HEY, VICTOR, EVERYBODY'S DATES ARE FLAKING ON THEM FOR THE DANCE...
...SO WE WERE WONDERING IF YOU WANTED TO COME WITH US AS A GROUP.
WELLIDON'TKNOWOKAYYES!
COOL, SEE YOU AT EIGHT!
YES!!! SAVED!
NO DATES MEANS I CAN DANCE WITH ALL THE CHICKS TONIGHT!
ALTHOUGH...
...MAYBE JUST ONE WOULD BE BETTER...
poit

(Theme from A Summer Place)
VICTOR...?
YES, CLOVER?
AH... I WAS WONDERIN'... COULD YOU POSSIBLY...
YES??
GRAB ME FEKKIN' ARSE ANY HARDER?
WHAT, ARE YOU TRYING TO DRAW BLOOD OR SOMETHIN', YA PERVERT?!?
GRR
SQUISH!
OH, SORRY...
YEAH, EXACTLY.
LIKE I COULD EVER PIERCE THAT ROCK SHE HAS FOR A HEART! HA!
AND SO...
PRIMAL
AM
OADED
DID YOU GET A HOLD OF THEM?
I GOT VICTOR, BUT CLOVER WASN'T HOME.
HER DAD SAID SHE WAS GONE WHEN HE GOT THERE AND HAS NO IDEA WHERE SHE'S OFF TO...
SHIT! IS VICTOR COMING?
YEAH, HE'LL BE THERE.
MAYBE CLOVER CHANGED HER MIND AND IS GOING AFTER ALL.
IF SHE DOESN'T MEET US HERE, I KNOW SHE'LL TURN UP AT THE DANCE.
SHE HAS TO!
WHY DOES IT MATTER SO MUCH?
I DON'T KNOW!
I THINK IT JUST DOESN'T FEEL RIGHT DOING STUFF WITHOUT HER AROUND.
HMPH.
LIKE IT'S SACRILEGE OR SOMETHING!

8:30 PM ROLLS AROUND...
JHS

'SUP?
I THOUGHT CLOVER WAS COMING?

I WAS HOPING SHE WOULD, BUT WE COULDN'T GET A HOLD OF HER.
I'M BUMMED TOO, COS NOW I HAVE NO ONE TO MAKE FUN OF ALL THE SLOBBERY COUPLES WITH!
YOU CALLED HER HOUSE?
YEAH, ERIN DID. CLOVER'S DAD DIDN'T KNOW WHERE SHE WAS. I DUNNO, MAYBE SHE'LL STILL SHOW UP?
I DON'T CARE, I WAS JUST WONDERING...

8:45
HAPPY VALENTINE'S DAY!

9:00
HAPPY VALENTINE'S DAY!

9:15
HAPPY VALENTINE'S DAY!

YOU OKAY?
VWP
THIS DANCE SUCKS.
I'M GONNA GO SEE IF I CAN FIND CLOVER.

THERE'S ONLY SO MANY PLACES SHE CAN HIDE...

WHEN IN ROME
"THE PROMISE"
I'M SORRY BUT I'M JUST THINKING OF THE RIGHT WORDS TO SAY--
--I KNOW THEY DON'T SOUND THE WAY I PLANNED THEM TO BE--
LUCKY
URGER
--BUT IF I HAD TO WALK THE WORLD I'D MAKE YOU FALL FOR ME, I PROMISE YOU--
--I PROMISE YOU, I WILL--
OAK HILL
EMETER
PIZZA FACTORY
HELLO, MR. CONNOLLY? THIS IS VICTOR.
IS CLOVER THERE?
NO, I'M AFRAID I DON'T KNOW WHERE SHE'S OFF TO.
WASN'T THERE A DANCE TONIGHT?
DON'T F
WITH TH
COOK
DEADWOOD COMMUNITY PARK

DUH! MEYERS! *
* MEYERS IS WHERE THE GANG SWIMS AND PICNICS IN THE SPRING. REALLY ANOTHER GENERAL YEAR-ROUND HANGOUT.

PLINK

MAYBE I SHOULDA GONE ANY-WAY.
I SHOULDA JUST SAID "SURE" TO THAT FOOL, EVEN IF HE WOULD HAVE RATHER ASKED BLEU OR ERIN FIRST.
PLINK

IT'D SAVE ME FROM FEELIN' LIKE THIS, THAT'S FOR CERTAIN.

PLUNK

OH...!

GOD-- GET A HOLD OF YOURSELF, MAN.
PLINK

OKAY.

HMM.

PUNK

SPLOOSH

SWEET SUFFERIN' FUCK THAT'S *COLD!!*

YOU USELESS BASTARD!

YEAH, YOU ASSHOLE! BETTER RUN! SHE'LL KICK YOUR ASS FOR THAT SHIT!

PUSSY!

SHOWED HIM. CAN YOU BELIEVE THAT GUY?

I CAN'T BELIEVE *THIS* ONE!

SORRY...

...DIDN'T MEAN FOR YOU TO GET ALL WET LIKE THAT.

WHAT'D YOU THINK WOULD HAPPEN, THEN?

I DUNNO, JUST THOUGHT IT'D BE FUNNY.

JUST... TRYING TO GET YOUR ATTENTION.

...
...

VICTOR...?

WHAT WOULD YOU DO IF I KISSED YOU RIGHT NOW?

I... DUNNO, PROBABLY FALL OFF THIS BRIDGE OR SOMETHING...

I'M THAT GROSS TO YOU, AM I?

JAYSUS, YOU GUYS REALLY SEE ME AS SOME REVOLTING, HEARTLESS--
WAIT, I DIDN'T MEAN IT LIKE THAT--

.02 NANOSECONDS LATER.
I THINK I SEE THEM UP AHEAD!
ZOOM
JESUS, IT'S COLD AS HELL OUT HERE, YOU GUYS!
WH-WHAT ARE YOU DOING HERE?
ERIN THOUGHT WE SHOULD HELP VICTOR FIND YOU.
YEAH, IT'S WAY TOO FREEZING TO BE OUT HERE ALL NIGHT.
WE SHOULD GO SOMEWHERE WARM TO HANG OUT.
UHH, SURE...
Y-YEAH, UH, WASN'T THERE A DANCE TONIGHT?
YAY! 'BOUT TIME YOU CAME TO YOUR SENSES!
COME ON, CHICKIE BABY, LET'S GO SHAKE IT!

♪
BLEU, YOU HAVE THE SQUAREST VOCABULARY ON THE PLANET.
YOU'RE THE ONE WHO SAID "SQUARE". WHO USES THAT ANYMORE?
I WAS USING IT TO MAKE A POINT!
ERIN, YOU'RE SO *RAD*.
SO *BOSS*.
SO MUCH HIPPER THAN ME.

SHUT UP!
YEAH, BLEU. PUT A LID ON IT, DADDIO!
THE KINKS
HAPPY VALENTINE'S DAY, KIDS!
ALL THIS DIPPY LOVE CRAP IS MAKING ME ILL.

"Nobody's Fool"

PETE MURPHY

everything's gone green

by CHYNNA
CLUCKIN'
CHICKEN '03

THAT'S *NANCY*, YOU TWAT!!!
YOU CHANGED YOUR NAME TO NANCY?
JEFFERSON
MOON SKA
BONK
YIPE!
WELL, CLOVER DID BEAT THE SHIT OUT OF HALF OF JEFFERSON HIGH'S MALE POPULATION BEFORE THE FIRST BELL...
HER KNUCKLES ARE JUST TOO SORE RIGHT NOW FOR HER TO PUNCH THE DORK BRIGADE AGAIN, AND THEY KNOW IT!
ALAN'S TOOTH WAS THE KICKER... I THINK I BROKE SOMETHIN' ON THE LITTLE BASTARD.
WHAT DID YOU EXPECT ON A DAY LIKE TODAY? YOU AREN'T WEARING ANY GREEN!
I AM SO! LOOK!
FRONT 242
IT'S AMAZING. ALL IRISH MUST HAVE INHERITED ST. PATRICK'S GIFT.
WHAT'S THAT?
DRIVING SNAKES OUT OF PLACES! LOOK, YOU DROVE THE SNAKES OUT OF OUR PANTS!
SHRIEK!
ZZZIP!
OH, GAD, NANCY!!! WHY DO YOU HURT ME SO?!
Nosebleed
WHERE IS THE TENDERNESS?

And so...
THANK THE GODS FOR LUNCHTIME!
INDEED. IT'S THE ONLY PART OF THE DAY WHEN THOSE PRICKS SHUT UP FOR A WHILE.
TOO BAD IT'S NORMALLY OUR LUNCHES THEY'RE EATING...
YARM
YARM
THEY'RE TOO BUSY STUFFING THEIR FAT FACES!
Soon after the stuffing of the fat faces...
WHAT'S THAT?
ISN'T IT OBVIOUS? IT'S MY PET SHAMROCK!
YOUR PET SHAMROCK.
YEAH. I THINK HE'S CUTE. I'M GOING TO KEEP HIM. LOOK, HE HAS A LITTLE FACE.
ARE YOU SERIOUS? YOU'RE SUCH A GIRL!
YOU CAN HAVE A PET SHAMROCK, TOO! HERE, PICK ONE.
KEEP YOUR LITTLE WEEDS TO YOURSELF, GOMEZ.
YOU'LL CHANGE YOUR MIND, WAIT AND SEE. I'LL JUST PUT THESE RIGHT IN HERE FOR YOU, FOR WHEN YOU REALIZE HOW MUCH YOU WISH YOU HAD ONE.
UH-OH, DON'T LOOK NOW, IT'S LABELLEPHANT...
CONNELLY! I WANT TO SEE YOU IN MY OFFICE THIS INSTANT!
I ADMIT NOTHING!

YOU SEEM TO BE UNAWARE THAT WE DON'T TOLERATE VIOLENT BEHAVIOR AT JEFFERSON HIGH!
I THINK YOU'D BETTER COME WITH ME SO WE CAN DISCUSS YOUR SUSPENSION. I HAVE RELIABLE WITNESSES TO YOUR BRUTALITY!
IT'S NOT MY FAULT THE FOOTBALL TEAM CAN'T HANDLE A FEW BUSTED RIBS, THE SISSIES!
MOVE IT, YOUNG LADY!
HANDS OFF, CHUNK!
WHAT'S THAT!?
HUH?
ILLEGAL SUBSTANCES, CONNELLY?? DON'T YOU KNOW THIS IS A DRUG FREE ZONE?!
BUT THEY'RE JUST STUPID SHAMROCKS, SIR!
WE'LL SEE ABOUT THAT, MISSY!
STOMP STOMP STOMP
LOOKS LIKE WE'LL BE DISCUSSING YOUR EXPULSION INSTEAD! LET'S GO!
DID THAT JUST HAPPEN?
BUT, BUT, BUT...!
HA-HA-HA-HA!!! CLOVER'S GONNA GET EXPELLED FOR "POSSESSION OF CLOVER"!
THEY'RE SHAMROCKS, YOU ASS! GET IT STRAIGHT!
Somewhere around 3:15 PM...
WOW, YOU'RE ALIVE! WHAT'S THE DEAL?
ARE YOU REALLY GETTING EXPELLED OVER VICTOR'S LITTLE FRIENDS?
SUSPENDED, ANYWAY!
THEY'RE ACTUALLY SENDING IT TO A LAB TO BE TESTED, AND UNTIL IT'S PROVEN TO NOT BE SOME SORT OF FOKIN' COCAPEYOTEMARIJUANA PLANT, I CAN'T COME BACK TO FEKKIN' SCHOOL! THIS IS TYRRANY!
I KNEW LABELLEPHANT WAS DUMB, BUT I HAD NO IDEA HE WAS THAT DUMB!
8

YOU'RE NOT GOING TO GET IN TROUBLE AT HOME, ARE YOU?
NAH, ME DA WILL THINK LABELLEPHANT IS THE ONE ON DRUGS. HE KNOWS I'VE NOTHING TO DO WITH THAT SHITE.
AGH! I HATE THIS FEKKIN' SCHOOL! AND I HATE THIS FEKKIN' HOLIDAY! NOTHING GOOD EVER HAPPENS TO ME ON THIS DAY!
BUT, CLOVER! IT'S ST. PATRICK'S DAY! IT'S ABOUT FOOD AND MUSIC AND BEER AND...FOOD!
YEAH, IRISH FOOD... MUST BE WHY THEY DRINK MORE THAN EAT...
FOOOOD.
WHAT COULD BE BETTER THAN THAT? I MEAN, EXCEPT THE BEER PART, COS I HAVE TO WAIT 'TIL I'M 21 TO HAVE ANY. BUT WHEN I CAN, I MEAN, WOW! PARTY 'TIL YOU PUKE!
ST. PATRICK CAN GET STUFFED! I'M GOIN' HOME, AND I'M GOIN' TO BED!
MAN, IS SHE IN FOR A SURPRISE.
GOD, WHAT SHOULD I WEAR TO THE PARTY, ANYWAY?
ERIN, GO BRALESS!!!
sorry! just had to get that one out of the way!
HULLO, CLO--
SLAM
T' HELL WITH EVERYONE! I'M GOING TO SLEEP UNTIL THIS BLOODY HOLIDAY IS OVER!
GOOD NIGHT!

Just a wee bit later...
WOO! YEAH, PAAARTY! BRING ON THE PIT BEEF 'N' LETTUCE!
THAT'S CORNED BEEF AND CABBAGE, YOU NINNY!
THAT, TOO!
THE ALARM - "THE STAND"

MAD WORLD
WHAT THE FUCK!?

ZOOM!
WHAT'S WITH ALL THE NOISE?!?
THERE SHE IS!

...in her underwear! thank you, god!
VWP

DA! WHAT'S GOIN' ON?!
I INVITED EVERYONE I THOUGHT YOU'D PROBABLY LIKE TO HAVE OVER FOR TH' PARTY SINCE I KNOW YOU'RE TOO LAZY TO DO IT.
too bad we couldn't make bloody mary sundaes! >snort<
BUT, DA!
SHUT IT AND BE A GOOD HOSTESS!

HOSTESS SHMOSTESS! SOMEBODY GIVE ME A MACHETE!
AW, CHEER UP, CLOVER. WE'RE HERE TO SHOW YOU A GOOD TIME!
C'MON, HAVE SOME PUNCH. IT'S REALLY TASTY. AND SORTA CHEWY.
MAD WORLD

OPEN MY MOUTH AND OUT POPS SOMETHING SPITEFUL

I REALLY WANT SOME MORE PUNCH, BUT SHE'S SCARING ME!
MAD WORL
I HATE TODAY, I HATE TODAY, I HATE TODAY...
...DANNY BOY!

oh danny boooooy, the pipes, the pipes are caaaaaaallling...!
NO, NO, NO, NO!

from glen to glennnnn, and doooooown the mountain siiiiide!
Give me back me Lucky Charms!
GOD ABOVE, KILL ME NOW...

!!!

SHLURP
MAD WORLD

the summer's goooooone and all the leaves are faaaalling...

WHOA, CLOVER, SAVE SOME PUNCH FOR US! YOU ALMOST DOWNED THE WHOLE THING!

URRGH... I'M GONNA BE SICK...
WIPE 'EM

BLEEEAAGH
ZIP!
MAD WOR

UGGGH.
HOY! Y'VOMITED IN ME CASHBOX!
ME POT O' GOLD!

HUH?
YOUR *WHAT?*
SHOO, SHOO! OFF WITH YE, BEHEMOTH!
POP!

ACH, *LEPRECHAUNS?!* I DON'T EVEN BELIEVE IN YOU BASTARDS!
WHAT THE HELL IS GOING ON??
YOU SHOULD KNOW THAT BY NOW! IT'S WHAT WE DO EVERY ST. PATRICK'S DAY IN THESE PARTS! WE GROUP TOGETHER FOR PROTECTION FROM ROVING, GOLD-HUNTIN' HUMANS AND SELL OUR WARES AT THE SAME TIME...
It's very practical.
Yes, very practical.
IT'S THE Northern California Annual Leprechaun Convention!
A.K.A. *LEPRECON!*

HUAAARCH
AGH! NOT AGAIN! GO AWAY!
PTOO... PTOO! GOD... WHY ME?
MAD WOR

SHOVE
THERE YOU ARE! YOU'RE LATE! COME WITH US!
MAD WORLD
SHOVE

YICK! DON'T FOKIN' TOUCH ME, YOU WADDLING BOOGER!
SO? WE LIKE 'EM THAT WAY!
ACH, SHE'S DRUNK!

AYE, I SUPPOSE IT'S TRUE--ELVES GET SO EASY WHEN THEY'RE ON THE SAUCE...!
I HEARD THAT, PRICK! AND I'M NOT AN ELF, I'M HUMAN!
SAME DIFFERENCE, JUST TWICE AS EASY!
MAD WORLD
SAY THAT AGAIN IN ARM'S REACH, Y'FOK--
COME ALONG, COME ALONG... WE DON'T 'AVE ALL NIGHT!

WHERE ARE WE GOING?!
TO THE CHANGING ROOM! DON'T EXPECT TO GET PAID IF YOU DON'T DO YER JOB!
MY JOB? WHAT BLOODY JOB?

UGH--HOW CAN YOU FORGET? YOU'RE THE GRATUITOUS BUSTY ELVEN LEPRECOMIX MASCOT! NOW PUT THIS ON, AND BE QUICK ABOUT IT!
JUST A SECOND, SHOULDN'T YOU HAVE A FEMALE LEPRECHAUN BE THE MASCOT OF LEPRECOMIX?
AN' I TOLD YOU I'M NOT AN ELF, ALREADY!
HAVE YOU EVER SEEN A CUTE AND BUSTY LEPRECHAUN?

WELL, NO...
VWOOM
EXACTLY! NOW GET IN THERE!

...BOSS ME AROUND, UGLY LITTLE KNOB-EATIN'...
WHAT TH' HELL ARE LEPRECHAUNS DOIN' OUT OF IRELAND, ANYWAY...?

ON SECOND THOUGHT, TAKE YOUR TIME.
REALLY.

FEK AFF!!!
WHY AM I ALWAYS SURROUNDED BY SEXUAL DEVIANTS? EVERYWHERE I GO! PERVERTS, PERVERTS!
HOY, YOU ACTUALLY EXPECT ME T'WEAR THIS TRASH? IT DOESN'T EVEN FIT, AND MY UNDERWEAR IS SHOW-ING!
LOOKS GOOD TO US.
WHEN YOU GO OUT TO THE BOOTH AND PRANCE AROUND, BE SURE TO HAVE MORE OF A BOUNCE IN YOUR WALK, RIGHT?
MUISE! HA HA HA HA HA HA HA
BUT, DONEL! SHE MIGHT GET A BLACK EYE IF SHE DOES!
WATCH IT, YOU GREEN TUBBA LARD...
*MUISE = INDEED
OH, WE'RE WATCHING!
Y'KNOW, SEAN, I WOULD TRADE ALL THE GOLD IN THE KINGDOM OF FAE JUST TO HAVE ONE STAB AT THAT WITH MY SHILELAGH!
SO WOULD WE!
HA HA HA! BWAA HAA HA!
TÁ GO MAITH*, THAT DOES IT! Y'BASTARDS ARE FEKKIN' DEAD!
*TÁ GO MAITH = ALRIGHT
YOU'RE ALL JUST LIKE EVERY BOY I EVER MET-- HORNY AND WORTHLESS! DIE!!!
IT'S A PSYCHOBILLY FREAKOUT!

MASH
MASH MASH
MASH
MASH
ZING!
MASH
MASH
MASH
MASH
Yiiii! NOOO!
HEY, SHE'S OVER HERE!
AND SHE'S BEATING THE SHIT OUT OF ALL OF THE NEIGHBORS' *LAWN GNOMES!!!*
WELL, BRING HER BACK OVER HERE QUICK, BEFORE THEY GET HOME!

GASP
HA-HA-HA!!! ...YOU OKAY, CLOVER?
HACK
GASP
...AND WHAT ARE YOU BEATING UP THE MCKEEVERS' YARD DECOR FOR?

HUH? *YARD DECOR?* AH, CHRIST! I THOUGHT THEY WERE A BUNCHA KNOB'EAD LEPRECHAUNS!
WHOAAA... LOOKS LIKE ALAN WAS RIGHT ABOUT PUTTING THE WHOLE BOTTLE OF BAILEY'S IN THE PUNCH! AWESOME!
MAD WORLD
COME ON, WE GOTTA GO. YOU'RE ON MY TEAM!

YOUR TEAM? BUT... WHAT ABOUT BLEU...?
WHAT ABOUT HER? IT'S ME AN' YOU, LET'S GO!

AND GUESS WHAT? WE SAVED THE BEST PART FOR LAST!!
OH, BOY. I JUST *CAN'T* WAIT.
MAD WORLD

HERE YOU GO!
'BOUT TIME!
WE WENT TO A LOT OF TROUBLE AND MADE SOMETHING FOR YOU SPECIAL, CLOVER, IN HONOR OF YOUR *GLORIOUS* HERITAGE.
YOU CAN THINK OF IT AS OUR WAY OF SAYING "SORRY" FOR YOUR PERSECUTION THIS AFTERNOON, AND IN TURN, OF YOUR PEOPLE FOR THE PAST 800 YEARS.

YOU SEE, WE THOUGHT IT ONLY APPROPRIATE-- SINCE ALL IRISH GIRLS ARE LUSHES-- THAT WE MAKE YOU A CUSTOM "PADDY WAGON" SO WE COULD GET YOU HOME WITHOUT YOU HARMING ANYONE, INCLUDING YOURSELF!
¡SQUEAL!
PADDY WAGON!
A GREEN SHOPPING CART?
BUT I LIVE HERE! I DON'T *NEED* A RIDE HOME!
PADDY WAGON!
YEAH, WELL, WE'RE MAKING A BIT OF A DETOUR BEFORE WE ACTUALLY LET YOU GO HOME.
HA-HA-HA! HAVE FUN, CLOVER! I'M GLAD TO SAY MY SHOPPING CART DAYS ARE OVER!
OH, YOU THINK SO?
DON'T WORRY, BLEU. WE'RE NOT LEAVING ANY OF YOU GIRLS OUT OF THE FUN. YOU ALL HAVE YOUR VERY OWN CART TO ENJOY AS WELL!
REPEAT THAT?
WE'RE AFRAID YOU NEED SEAT BELTS, HOWEVER.
IT'S FOR YOUR SAFETY.
LIKE HELL! WE'RE OUTTA HERE!
THREE MINUTES LATER.
RATTA RATTA RATTA RATTA RATTA R
DAMN, WHEN'D THEY GET SO FAST? WE EVEN HAD A HEAD START.
IT'S A SCIENTIFICALLY PROVEN FACT THAT ALL HORNY CREEPS RUN QUICKER THAN ANY NORMAL HUMAN BEING CAN MANAGE. HENCE, OUR DIRE SITUATION.
PADDY WAGON!
U2 - "PRIDE (IN THE NAME OF LOVE")*
OKAY, NOW, LET'S SEE HOW FAST THEY FLY DOWN LILLEY MOUNTAIN!
...SIGH...
MY THOUGHTS EXACTLY. START ON THOSE "OUR FATHERS" AND "HAIL MARYS," GIRLS. YOU'RE GONNA NEED 'EM!
*song selections not endorsed by Oni editorial staff (namely Jamie)
Happy St. Pat's, y'brats.

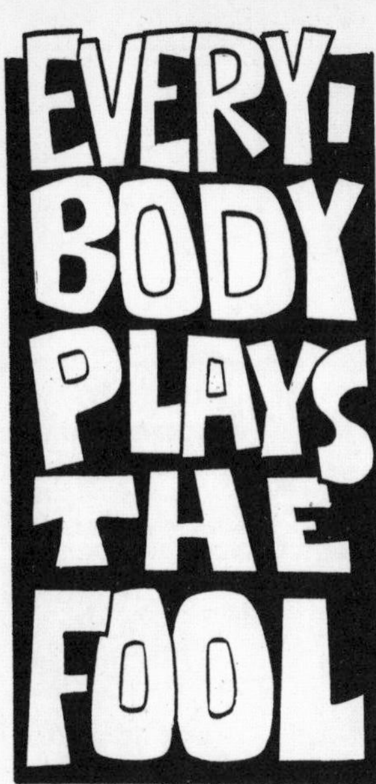

A BLUE MONDAY COMIC
BY CHYNNA CLUGSTON-MAJOR!

SUNDAY, 11:59 P.M.
OHHHH...
MY YOUTH... IT'S PASSING BEFORE MY EYES...
SCOOTER BABE
CHECKMATE
CONCRETE BLONDE - "HAPPY BIRTHDAY"

MY PRECIOUS TEENAGE YEARS ARE QUICKLY SLIPPING AWAY, AND ONE DAY SOON, I'M GOING TO WAKE UP AND BE TWENTY-EIGHT...
MARCH
AND THEN WHAT WILL LIFE HAVE TO OFFER, I ASK?
RUDIE CAN'T FAIL

NOTHING, NOTHING! I'LL BE OLD AND INFIRM, WITH ONE FOOT IN THE GRAVE!
MY B-DAY!

OH, TO BE YOUNG AND CARELESS AGAIN... JUST LIKE IN THE GOOD OLD DAYS...
...'BOUT A YEAR OR SO AGO.
DREDD

"SATURDAY"
LGB
8:00 PM
SIIIIGH.
PRINCE BUSTER
RUDIE CAN'T FAIL
HALLOWEEN
?
Been Sitting there since November
HALLOWEEN
Costume Stuff
AH, THE REMNANTS OF MY BYGONE, BAUHAUS ERA...
RUDIE CAN'T FAIL
HALLOWEEN
RUDIE
the beat
...
LGB
heh...

OKAY, WE'LL SEE IF VICTOR'S STILL UP. IF HE ISN'T, WE'LL JUST GO BACK TO ERIN'S AND GO TO BED.
NO, IF VICTOR'S ASLEEP, WE'LL WAKE HIS ASS UP AND MAKE HIM COME OUT WITH US WHETHER HE WANTS TO OR NOT.
IT'S AFTER MIDNIGHT, GOTTA START HIS BIRTHDAY OFF RIGHT!
COOL, HIS LIGHT IS ON!
LUCKY FOR HIM!
THE CRUXSHADOWS - "CRUELTY"
HAPPY BIRFDAY, YOU BIG APRIL FOO-- *AGH!!!!!!!!*
oh, my goff.
HEY!
I DON'T THINK WE WERE SUPPOSED TO SEE THAT!
WHAT, WAS HE SPANKING IT?! WAS HE NAKED? WHAT'D YOU SEE?
FWP
COME ON, AND I'LL TELL YOU! HA-HA-HA!!!
BUT I WANT TO SEE! I MEAN, NOT IF HE WAS NAKED OR SPANKING IT OR ANYTHING, BUT--
WAIT, *COME BACK!*
I CAN EXPLAIN!!!

OH, SHIT! SHIT SHIT SHIT! ...I'LL NEVER LIVE THIS DOWN!
I GOTTA THINK OF SOMETHING TO TELL THEM SO THEY DON'T SPREAD IT ALL OVER SCHOOL... THINK, THINK!
COME ON... THERE'S GOTTA BE SOMETHING I CAN- HM...?
...WAIT A SEC'.
APRIL
WELLLL, THERE'S NO WAY I CAN KEEP THEM FROM TELLING EVERYONE, THAT MUCH I SHOULD KNOW BY NOW... BUT MAYBE I CAN HAVE THE UPPER HAND IN THIS AFTER ALL!
HEH-HEH...
APRIL
THE CURE - "LULLABYE"
COME MONDAY MORNING...
YOU'RE KIDDING! IN MAKE-UP?
HA HA HA!
...LOOKING ALL DEATH ROCKER!
WAIT, WHO'S *THAT?*
JUST LIKE ROBERT SMITH!
NO WAY...

VICTOR?!?!
HA HA HA!
NUH-UH!

WOW, YOU DO LOOK LIKE ROBERT SMITH! HEE-HEE!
FOR YOU.
OOOOH, YOU'RE SO *PREEETTY!* HA-HA-HA-HA!!! >GASP, CHOKE<

Sniff
SHLURP
AND YOU, AND YOU...
HEH-HEH... EH-HEH...

...AND FOR YOU.
...

SIGH.
!

WOBBLE WOBBLE
HEY!

ECHO AND THE BUNNYMEN - "BEDBUGS AND BALLYHOO"
WHAT'S THE BIG IDEA? YOU GOING RETARDED IN YOUR OLD AGE?
WHATEVER DO YOU MEAN?
PETER MURPHY
THIS!
I THOUGHT YOU GREW OUT OF THAT WHINY-ASSED "CRAWL-INTO-A-CORNER-AND-LISTEN-TO-DEPRESSED-MODE, PATHETIC, POETRY-WRITIN', ALL-BLACK-WEARIN', PULLIN'-TAFFY-INSTEAD-OF-DANCIN'" PHASE! I MEAN, HONESTLY, I WAS *HOPING* YOU'D GET OUT OF THAT DUMB RUDEBOY SKA-DORK HOMO PHASE, TOO, BUT I WAS FIGURING YOU'D GO MOD INSTEAD OF USING THE WAY-BACK MACHINE TO TAKE YOU HOME TO SNIVEL-LAND!
PETER MURPHY
WELL, IT'S HERE TO STAY. THIS IS THE *REAL ME*, ALAN, AND I'M JUST NOT GOING TO HIDE IT ANYMORE. REJECT ME IF YOU WILL, JUST LIKE EVERYONE ELSE HAS!
YOUR EYELINER IS CROOKED, YOU PUSSY!
SOB
IDIOT.
THE KINKS
BODDINGTON
HA-HA-HA! HE WENT FOR IT! THIS IS SO GREAT. I CAN DO ANYTHING AND NOT EVEN BE EMBARASSED ABOUT IT, BECAUSE IT'S NOT REALLY ME ANYMORE!
I WONDER WHAT ELSE I COULD GET AWAY WITH?

MORRISSEY - "THE LAST OF THE FAMOUS INTERNATIONAL PLAYBOYS"
NICE LIPSTICK, FAG!
YEAH, FAG!

I'M SO MISUNDERSTOOD! WHY...? WHYEEEE?!?
GOMEZ! SHUT UP AND BLOCK THE BALL!
GOOD ONE, DUDE.
I KNOW!

WHY-HAI-HAI-HAIIIII?!?
JHS GYM

WHYYYYYYYYYYYYYYYY?!
SHOOM

SLAM!
whimper

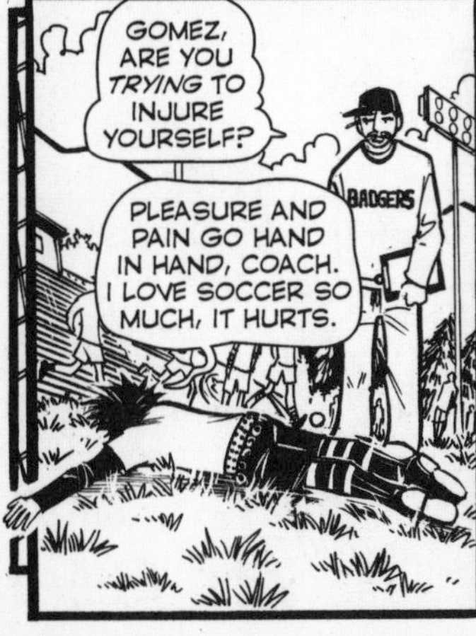
GOMEZ, ARE YOU *TRYING* TO INJURE YOURSELF?
BADGERS
PLEASURE AND PAIN GO HAND IN HAND, COACH. I LOVE SOCCER SO MUCH, IT HURTS.

YOU SURE HE'S NOT JOKING?
NOPE. HE'S LOST IT.

Sometimes I really wonder what the hell Martin Gore is wearing, and why...

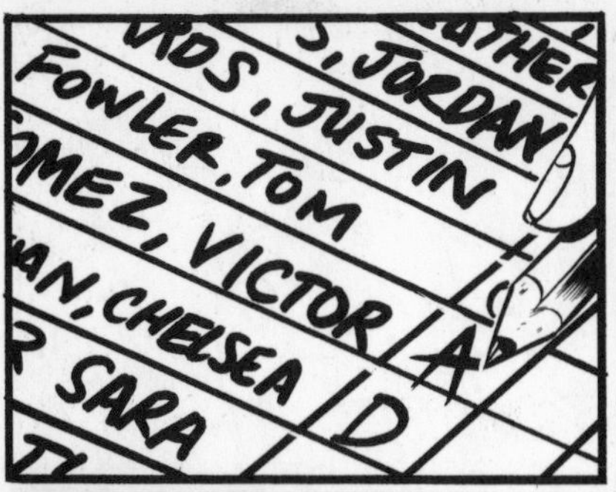
S, JORDAN
FOWLER, JUSTIN
OMEZ, TOM
VICTOR
AN, CHELSEA
SARA
A
D

That prick... that wasn't even the assignment!

EW.

DIDN'T ANYONE TELL HIM HALLOWEEN WAS LIKE, SIX MONTHS AGO?
YEAH, AND WHAT'S WITH THE CLOWN FACE, ANYWAY?
OH, MY.

LOOKING LOVELY TODAY, LADIES.

AND WHAT'S THAT SCENT? ...MMM. HEAVEN!
Sniff

IT KIND OF WORKS, THOUGH, DOESN'T IT?
YEAH... KIND OF *MYSTERIOUS*, ISN'T HE...

RUSTLE
RUSTLE
RUSTLE
?
VICTOR, WHAT ARE YOU DOING?
JIMMY'Z
I'M GOING TO LEAP FROM THIS TREE AND *END IT ALL!*
PETER MURPHY
END ALL OF WHAT? YOUR DAYS OF WALKING ON TWO LEGS? DON'T BE A RETARD, AND COME DOWN HERE.
NO! NEVER!
I HAVE YOUR BIRTHDAY PRESENT FOR YOU.
SNAP!
KRAK
OOH! A PRESENT? WAIT RIGHT THERE, JUST LET ME-
OWWWW....
NICE DIVE, MR. COUSTEAU.

THE NEXT DAY...
HEY, WHAT HAPPENED TO YOUR GOING BACK TO DEATH ROCK?
YEAH, RIGHT!
SEE, I KNEW IT. POSEUR!
WHAT'S WITH THEM?
YOU STARTED A TREND.
ALL THEIR GIRLFRIENDS WERE PROBABLY TALKING ABOUT YOU SO MUCH, I THINK THEY FIGURED THE ONLY WAY TO GET THEIR ATTENTION BACK WAS TO IMITATE YOU!
KMFD
DOI! IT WAS AN APRIL FOOL'S JOKE! LOOK WHO GETS THE LAST LAUGH, SUCKERS! HA-HA-HA!!!
I WOULDN'T LAUGH TOO HARD, VICTOR, COS IT ISN'T GONNA BE YOU.
UH.... SORRY?
LUNCH HOUR.
WHAT HAPPENED TO VICTOR?
HE GAVE A BUNCH OF CHICKS THE SAME STUPID LOVE POEM AND THEY HAPPENED TO COMPARE NOTES. THE DUMMY PROBABLY THOUGHT IF HE SLIPPED A COPY TO EVERY GIRL HE CAME ACROSS, AT LEAST ONE WOULD BE LAME ENOUGH TO ASK HIM OUT!
POUT
POUT
POUT

Don't change that channel! *Blue Monday* will be right back after issue six of my new series, *Scooter Girl!* See you then...

HAPPY BIRFDAY, JON!

SOMEWHERE IN MARCH...
HEY. ISN'T TODAY A HOLIDAY?
YEAH. I THINK IT'S ARBOR DAY OR SOMETHING.
ARBOR DAY? HOW THE HELL DO YOU CELEBRATE ARBOR DAY?
MMM... GOOOOD TREEEEE
PAT PAT PAT PAT
WELL, THAT WAS FUN. LET'S DO IT AGAIN SOMETIME.
ZZZ

BONUS MATERIAL

originally cd... brainstorming with the cupid thing, I like the idea of B, A, & E as woodland spirits

THE FAX FILES

The following pages contain various elements for the book that Chynna shared with Oni via the glorious technology of facsimile!

LEFT: A *Lovecats* pin-up that was never completed, since the story ran a full issue.

BOTTOM LEFT: Drawing for the second *Blue Monday* t-shirt from Graphitti Designs.

BOTTOM RIGHT: Early sketches of the controversial Seamus.

Seamus!
Pweez?
I dunno if I want to add whiskers or not. Thinkin' not.

LEFT: A faxed message of sympathy to Jamie.

LOWER LEFT: Very rough pencils for the original cover to this book, featuring way more characters.

BOTTOM RIGHT: A nearly complete version.

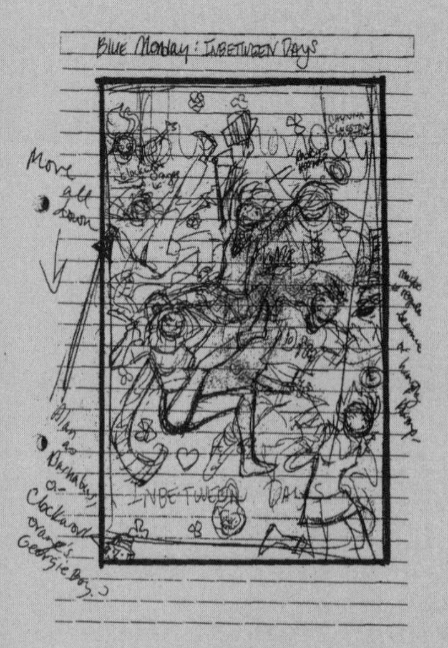

Cover to a split 7" single put out by Springman Records, featuring music by the Groovie Ghoulies and The Secretions. This was a Halloween release in 2002.

Chynna's drawing for a promotional magazine for a music distributor. We're not sure who all those characters are, either. She just made them up on the spot.

BLASTS FROM THE PAST!

Sketching out the cover for the second edition of *The Kids Are Alright*. Note the annotation in the lower right: "Two hours later I realize this is Britney's pose from her debut album. Fuck!!!" And what's wrong with that, we ask you?

LEFT: An early version of the cover for *Absolute Beginners* #1, borrowing the triptych design from The Jam's *The Gift* album cover, but not the poses—which is where we ultimately ended up.

BELOW: How it actually turned out.

blue monday
Hi! THIS IS RISSA! ... I WAS ASKED TO STEP IN FOR CHYNNA TODAY SINCE SHE'S STUCK DOING OTHER BLUE MONDAY STUFF... HOPE YOU LIKE MY COMIC! BYE!
HEY, LOOK, KIDS! IT'S APRIL FOOL'S DAY!
YEAH, I KNOW! AND IT'S MY BIRTHDAY!
Need I comment on this
We know! that's why we baked you a CAKE!
APRIL
TAKE A DEEP BREATH AND MAKE A WISH!
HOOORK!
NOT THAT DEEP, DUMMY!
SHOOM
URK! URK!
THWAP
PUA H!
SPLAT
HMM!
POKE
SLICE.
Chew Chew Chew
IT TASTES JUST FINE!
REALLY?
APRIL FOOLS!
EWWWWW!!!
EWWWW!
IT ACTUALLY TASTES JUST like Honey-glazed chicken!
(CAN WE WEAR A JOKE OUT, OR WHAT?)

Special Thanks to:

My big, beautiful, sassy-assed bully, Buster; as well as Guy Major; Dom Piper, Kaffy Clugston & Co; Mary Flores; Miss Momo and Jennay Sireci; Lissa Read (the whole Read family, really), Chris Denton-Cheese, all the Sacramento kids besides; Katie Bair, Lindsay; Nora; John Vidas?; Sas McSucky (aka Jamie McKelvie); Chris Siddall; Dax Balzer, Helen and The Uppers crew; Christine Norrie, Jen Van Meter and fam-fam; Scott and the kids at FanBoy Radio; Kevin Kieta (El Impo), Marco & the Worthing Mod-Crushers Club (and Evil Mark, their leader); The Pharaohs Scooter Club (San Diego chapter); Alex & Vespa Motorsport; Dan and Guillermo of The Secret Society S.C., Jenny Kay, Kim Schwenk, Andy Greenwald; Corey Henson; Michael Manzano (Mani who dances like a demon); the nice boys from HiFi; Nathan Matheney; The Regent Sound; Syd and Makoto; Donnie Gonzales, Mike Retro, Carol, and The Lips; Mr. Darcy; Rozzie and Josh; Jeanie, Christoph Melzer, Georg, Anna Mozer, Ehapa, Kitty Fukuyama, Michele Foschini, Mr. Wonderful, Keith Wood, Bryan O'Malley, Travis O'Neil, Benny, Dennis and Laarni, all those nice SF kids, Joe Nozemack, James and Jennie Jones, Intern Ian, Scott Morse, Evan and Sarah, Jim Mahfood, Jon Kovalic, Brian Glass, Shelly and Philip Bond, Matt Brady, Bob and Chip, Andi Watson, Daniel Krall, Lawrence Marvit, Craig Thompson (just 'cause he rules all), Judd Winick for many reasons, and lovely Pam, of course; Paul Dini, for letting us in the playground; all Oni friends and family; Your Mom, Ben's Mom, a million other people I'm spacing on right now thanks to sleep deprivation and corndog overload; but most of all Jon Flores for all the gag ideas and inspiration (especially on the St. Patrick's Day story, which we brainstormed one afternoon in downtown Disney after waaaay too many mint juleps),and to Jamie Rich, you evil, horrible thing. Much love.

Extra Special shout-out to Yosemite High's Class of 1993.
Ten years. TEN. TEN! YEARS! Go, Badgers.

— Chynna - San Diego, 2003

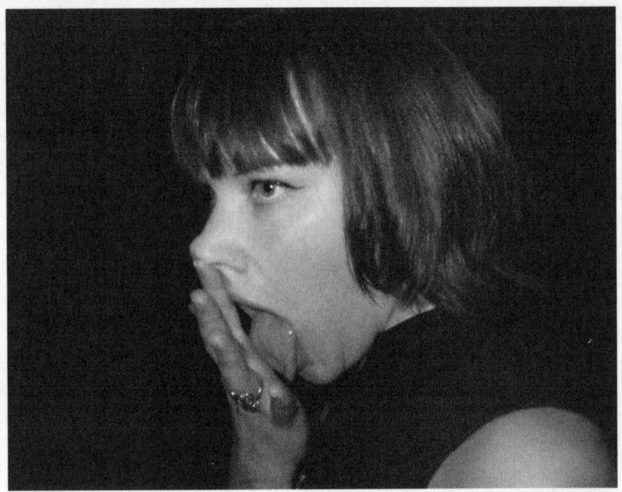

Chynna Clugston is the head of a sweat shop of specially trained bulldogs who have been bred to draw comic books. Led by top dog Buster, these gassy, pugfaced canines have now produced three volumes of *Blue Monday* and the stand-alone miniseries *Scooter Girl*.

When not mining the personal comedies and tragedies created by the hormones of American teenagers, Chynna's bulldogs lend their talent to other people's comics, using their ink-dipped claws and fangs to bring to life Paul Dini's *Jingle Belle*, the X-Men and Spider-Man in *Ultimate Marvel Team-Up*, the cast of *Buffy the Vampire Slayer* in the Dark Horse comics, Mike Allred's It Girl in *The Atomics: Spaced Out and Grounded in Snap City*, and Jen Van Meter's *Hopeless Savages*. Contrary to popular belief, they did not draw the illustrations in Jamie S. Rich's debut novel, *Cut My Hair*; Chynna drew those herself. (Awwwww...)

Given the free time she gains by letting her furry friends do her work, Chynna lives a life of leisure—watching Jack Lemmon movies while drinking Pepsi on the balcony of her spacious Southern California home. It doesn't suck to be her, nosirree.

Blue Monday will return with its fourth series in 2004. And the bulldogs don't plan to stop until they have all the sausage treats in the world.

Other books by Chynna Clugston & Oni Press...

BLUE MONDAY, VOL. 1: THE KIDS ARE ALRIGHT™
By Chynna Clugston
136 pages, $11.95 US
ISBN-10: 1-929998-62-7
ISBN-13: 978-1-929998-62-3

BLUE MONDAY, VOL 2: ABSOLUTE BEGINNERS™
By Chynna Clugston
128 pages, $11.95 US
ISBN-10: 1-929998-17-1
ISBN-13: 978-1-929998-17-3

BLUE MONDAY, VOL. 4: PAINTED MOON™
By Chynna Clugston
128 pages, $11.95 US
ISBN-10: 1-932664-11-4
ISBN-13: 978-1-932664-11-9

SCOOTER GIRL™
By Chynna Clugston
168 pages, $14.95 US
ISBN-10: 1-932664-88-0
ISBN-13: 978-1-929998-88-3

HOPELESS SAVAGES, VOL. 1™
By Jen Van Meter, Christine Norrie, & Chynna Clugston
136 pages, $11.95 US
ISBN-10: 1-929998-60-0
ISBN-13: 978-1-929998-60-9

HOPELESS SAVAGES, VOL. 2: GROUND ZERO™
By Jen Van Meter & Bryan Lee O'Malley w/ Chynna Clugston, Christine Norrie, & Andi Watson
128 pages, $11.95 US
ISBN-10: 1-929998-52-X
ISBN-13: 978-1-929998-52-4

LOST AT SEA™
By Bryan Lee O'Malley
168 pages, $11.95 US
ISBN-10: 1-932664-16-5
ISBN-13: 978-1-932664-16-4

SCOTT PILGRIM™, VOL. 1: SCOTT PILGRIM'S PRECIOUS LITTLE LIFE
By Bryan Lee O'Malley
168 pages, $11.95 US
ISBN-10: 1-932664-08-4
ISBN-13: 978-1-932664-08-9

SCOTT PILGRIM™, VOL. 2: SCOTT PILGRIM VS. THE WORLD
By Bryan Lee O'Malley
200 pages, $11.95 US
ISBN-10: 1-932664-12-2
ISBN-13: 978-1-932664-12-6

TWELVE REASONS WHY I LOVE HER™
By Jamie S. Rich & Joëlle Jones
144 pages, $14.95 US
ISBN-10: 1-932664-51-3
ISBN-13: 978-1-932664-51-5

Available at finer comic shops everywhere. For a comics store near you, call 1-888-COMIC-BOOK or visit www.the-master-list.com. For more Oni Press titles and information visit www.onipress.com